Theseus

His New Life

CAMILLE DE TOLEDO

Translated from the French
by Willard Wood

OTHER PRESS
NEW YORK

Originally published in French as *Thésée, sa vie nouvelle*
in 2020 by Éditions Verdier, Paris

Published by arrangement with Agence littéraire Astier-Pécher

Production editor: Yvonne E. Cárdenas
Text designer: Jennifer Daddio
This book was set in Filosofia by
Alpha Design & Composition of Pittsfield, NH

1 3 5 7 9 10 8 6 4 2

 Printed in the United States of America on
acid-free paper. For information write to Other Press LLC,
267 Fifth Avenue, 6th Floor, New York, NY 10016.
Or visit our Web site: www.otherpress.com

Library of Congress Cataloging-in-Publication Data
Names: Toledo, Camille de, 1976- author. | Wood, Willard, translator.
Title: Theseus, his new life / Camille de Toledo ; translated from
the French by Willard Wood.
Other titles: Thésée, sa vie nouvelle. English
Description: New York : Other Press, 2023. | Originally published in French as
Thésée, sa vie nouvelle in 2020 by Éditions Verdier, Paris.
Identifiers: LCCN 2022021011 (print) | LCCN 2022021012 (ebook) |
ISBN 9781635422108 (paperback) | ISBN 9781635422115 (ebook)
Subjects: LCGFT: Novels.
Classification: LCC PQ2720.O44 T4413 2023 (print) | LCC PQ2720.O44 (ebook) |
DDC 843/.92—dc23/eng/20220517
LC record available at https://lccn.loc.gov/2022021011
LC ebook record available at https://lccn.loc.gov/2022021012

Publisher's Note
This is a work of fiction. Names, characters, places, and
incidents either are the product of the author's imagination or
are used fictitiously.

PRAISE FOR

Theseus, His New Life

"Camille de Toledo is one of the most interesting and original young authors writing in French today. In his latest book—his most personal and his most historical—he casts himself as a modern Theseus, trapped in a labyrinth that is at once the story of a family blighted by its own legends, and a reckoning with a body crippled by ailments that medical science proves incapable of identifying. Toledo provides a moving account of a journey through the maze of his family's past."

—Ann Jefferson, author of *Nathalie Sarraute: A Life Between*

"*Theseus, His New Life* is family history on a societal scale. We are not just characters on the bounded stage where our visible life plays out. Our part has been written by others, our masks have been painted by those who accumulate and confiscate. But the film is full of jump cuts, continuity errors, some of the dialogue is missing, and throughout this fine book Camille de Toledo examines the seams of his family history, which are also those of modern capitalism and its supposed human face. He does this firmly but gently, determined to free himself, through sensitivity, thought, and language, from the doubtful prose of profit."

—Éric Vuillard, Goncourt Prize–winning author of *The Order of the Day*

"I have been reading and admiring the work of Camille de Toledo for over a decade. He is unique for his fidelity to the history of Europe and the history of Jewishness—and all the problems of maintaining that double fidelity. His writing is playful, somber, lyrical, and exact. *Theseus, His New Life* continues this examination of history and identity, but this time with a painfully personal inflection. A family is a history, this is the book's deep wisdom: but as well as being contaminated by the past it shows how we might disown our inheritance too."

—Adam Thirlwell, international bestselling author of *Politics*

"A beautiful text with the weight of a myth and the sadness of a dirge."

—*Le Monde*

"[De Toledo] explores the familial labyrinth, pulling us in with enchanting, captivating, harrowing prose."

—*La Croix*

"An incredible introspection, which sweeps through the history of the twentieth century and invites us to reflect profoundly on human destiny."

—Culturebox

The fathers have eaten sour grapes,

and the children's teeth are set on edge

EZEKIEL 18:2

my brother, tell me . . .

who commits the murder of a man who kills himself?

you were born January 26
nineteen seventy-three

a few months after your birth
came the first oil crisis
heralding the end of the world

of infinite energy

after thirty years of capitalism in free fall
you gave up your life
and I have been, since that day, your survivor
the one who carries on his back the riddle
of your death

a riddle that extends across eras

across borders
a loss and a gap tied to other
tales from the past that extend
a fragile thread

when I pull on this thread, here's what emerges:

that we are
a continuum of disasters
and collapses

and this envelope we call Body
that we wear, and care for, and worship is nothing but
crystallized links that may
in exile, or old age, or an accident
dissolve

a brother, a mother, a father, a language
the imprint of a city we have learned to love
the memory of a forest around
a village, in childhood

when we lose our links, my brother,
we fall

as after your death I fell

I was battered by, flooded with strange forces
from the past
no days for me
no light

I had to recover your faces, my family,
revisit the history that gave us birth

and to follow those forces, I had
to immerse myself again in those absurd,
amnesiac times

the *Trente Glorieuses*,
the thirty years of postwar prosperity

I then had to go through the war again, back to the
trenches
of that other century
dive into the waters of that time
illuminate the lies
we are the children of

my brother,
so as not to die I had to take a journey
into the heart of night, the folds of the body
the strata of time

to understand what took you

and answer the ugly question
which ended up overturning everything
that I believed, yes, me, the modern one

the child of prosperity

who commits the murder of a man who kills himself?

for with this question the archaic tale begins
slicing between the ages and ricocheting
from life to life, from the past to the future

the future

March 1,
two thousand five

PARIS

a father unknots alone the rope his son has used to
hang himself, I am in a taxi crossing the river, I know
nothing of what is happening, but the message on
my voice mail says to hurry, and it's a voice of terror,
the father's; I run from the taxi, enter a code on
the keypad, fumble it; hanging is an archaic action
unlike jumping out a window, the rope comes to us
from the past, I'll return to this; but for now I bolt
up the staircase, the treads are worn, the door to the
third floor is open, I see my father sitting; in a corner,
the brother stretched out

now everything is falling and life is accursed

the intuition I have had since childhood is finally
confirmed; I believe it now, at least I have the sense
that everything that's happening, the brother, the
father sitting, that everything is proceeding in
obedience to a law, an equation; the brother sprawled,
my approaching him; in that moment, a cry arises

from me to wrench him from death, from those who let their pains and secrets seep from body to body, year to year; and simultaneous with the cry arises the memory of our childhood, but the brother stays put on the red floor tiles; nothing wakes him, nothing can be repaired; a line is cut between the dead brother and the father, the mother, the brother who are still alive; and one image is missing, I'll search for it a long time; the image of the brother hanging

now everything is falling and life is accursed

and the image he leaves behind, the image that will haunt all who are left to restart their lives, is a devouring wound; then the firemen arrive, the mother, whom the father informed; her face when she enters is not something you remember; his face when they carry out the body is not something you look at; you look at nothing; you're with the father and the remaining brother; and this is where the block of feelings forms into a knot for the time that comes after; something clots in the heart, travels the bloodstream through the skin; a chemistry of fears whose effects will need deciphering if the future is to be woven of anything but ruins; what's left here is the father, the mother, and between them a fissure where the living brother breathes; the body of the dead brother, whose shoulders bore the burden of time, is carried off; the father, the mother, at this moment are not talking; there's silence and what is audible in silence; because when someone dies, it all turns into a morass of faults and remorse from which each tries to escape

now everything is falling and life is accursed

I realize that *from now on* life will be cut in two; and maybe I knew it from the start? maybe there is a coherence to everything that has happened? I'm going to have to hold it together, in the footsteps of the older brother, to carry this scene; the brother who is no more; from now on, I'll be the one remaining; and the days pass; visits from the family, from friends, are organized; people come to pay their respects to the mother; some, a bit embarrassed, manage to fold her in their arms; but on the whole it's a death that divides; the general sense is that nothing will be repaired; there are words already, out of the father and mother's hearing, trying to establish a narrative that will keep the body from disturbing others; he hadn't been well for years, he was ill, that's what's being said, what people want to believe; the family is looking for a narrative that will keep the suicide from contaminating life; it turns the story into a personal tragedy, a "free choice"; this stubborn myth that rises like a wall around the inner trembling for order's preservation; because the rope that links different eras and memories, the past and the future, no one wants it to reach all the way to them; the narrative—he was ill, for years he'd been unwell—is what's being used to draw a line between oneself and that

a brother who hangs himself

people voice their compassion; there's sadness and grief, for he was liked; his fragility in the end wore through his mantle of strength, which is the other name for power in this family; by sharing his pain, the brother who wanted to die—I sometimes think he *had* to die, and it's all tied up in that *having* to die, everything I am trying to understand—in the end moved others; he has made each person an orphan of hope, the hope of saving him; but who can come to his rescue when every mouth is hushed, when no one faces up to what's suppressed; people don't want the death to spatter them, so they establish a narrative; and this narrative comes to the mother's ears; what she feels is nothing she can share; she can't flee as she has done all her life; her son's suicide forces her to look at what she has pushed aside; and now it's too late, the son is gone and she says

I want to die

she says it to the son who is left; at night when I leave her, the mother looks for answers: *who commits the murder of a man who kills himself?* she asks, shutting herself in a forced sleep that deletes her; she still feeds on a powerful anger; she needs a culprit so as not to blame herself too much; hatred fills her, waves of it that she transmits to the living; the mother is a clenched fist that admits no light; she pretends to live, to eat, while behind these pretenses I see all that is crumbling; the mother is a cliff that terror is eroding; I stop by to see her, try to help; I am a hyphen between two worlds that are drawing apart: the continent of the living and the continent of the dead; I carry an intact hope, but life is dark; in the months following the brother's death, I become the father of my loved ones, the father of the mother and the father of the father

now everything is falling and life is accursed

a summer comes, when birds in a southern garden flit to and fro; one lands on the mother's shoulder; I say, by way of consolation, because I am trying to prove that life goes on, I say that the bird is the brother; the mother wants to believe it, she plays with the bird; then autumn days arrive, she resumes her work, or tries to; September comes and goes, October; the heavy skies of the Western city, gray roofs, pale colors, months and months when nothing repairs itself, everything worsens, the image is missing, the image of the son who hangs himself

where were you? what were you doing?

and there are the hours when you try to escape by resuming your routine; but the memory persists, the moment is unforgettable: the body of the son and the missing image of when he ropes up his neck, when he strains to breathe, when his blood stops; November comes and goes; "the brother has stolen the light from me, taken the sun," are the thoughts of the living brother when he sees that his strengths, his joys, are what sustains the others, especially the mother; and in fact the mother's head droops; she rests it on my shoulders for support; I stand still to steady her, and December ends, then January; she puts her trust in me, in what I seem to know: *I must transform the experience of this death or nothing will have any meaning*; and the mother senses that I've taken on this quest, but she wants a trial to be held over the suicide *who commits the murder of a man who kills himself?*

then everything slides downhill, accelerating; the mother's insistence on vengeance is carried forward into the future; it would take me years to understand what, in the months after the brother's death, flows from one body to another; and the month of January marks the birthday of the departed; the day is not one we celebrate; we see each other at lunch, the mother and I, to talk about ongoing life; we talk about the world, its wars, the one who died the previous March; the mother has just returned from a trip; she found the strength for this: to leave the Western city, autumn, the too-gray roofs, the wind in the perturbed streets; to take the plane, to sleep, to knock herself unconscious with pills and then to call me

do you want to have lunch?

we meet at place de la Bourse, in Paris, on an ordinary gray day; and it's January 26, the birthday of the dead son; but the birthday ritual has lost its meaning; we pretend to talk, say our goodbyes on the sidewalk; then in late afternoon the mother is discovered on a bus at the terminal sleeping for eternity; the day of the son's birth, the day of the mother's death thirty-three years apart; *on January 26*; and there will be other dates that intersect, "synchronicities," as they are called; or what are termed *coincidences* by those who stubbornly won't understand; but I call it a *lapsus tempi*, a slip of time, when the past joins with the future, when the definite outline of solid bodies wavers under what links names together from era to era; and the mother now is dead; the surviving son one evening crying says

soon I'll be the last one left

but he doesn't know where to address his prayer, and his father already is in decline; during the months between the brother's death and the mother's, the father came back, took care as best he could of family business; he helped choose materials for the caskets, shared his faith with me in an attempt to soothe: *I've spoken to your brother*, he said, *he is no longer suffering*, and now that the mother is dead, he adds: *she has found peace, believe me, she's with her son* . . . given his grief, how can I argue, and with what? reason? what reason? the brother who is left leaves his father to his beliefs, and if he talks to ghosts, to apparitions . . . everyone has to defend himself as he can; for we must now bid farewell to the mother and yet again call up the family, friends, acquaintances; the remaining brother greets, he organizes; till now he has lived behind the protection of his family; now it's up to him to hold strong, be a son who stands host; the father helps him, but the father is weakening, something is carrying him off; he is unable to counter those who establish a narrative for the mother's death; *she was devoured by guilt*, they say, *her son's death destroyed her, she wanted to die*; then there are those who offer their opinion: *she should have given her sons more breathing room*; and there are those who prudently say nothing; afterward, I see this, family and friends resume their lives; they feel sorrow, but life goes on and tragedy doesn't really have a place nowadays; and so the father and the remaining brother find themselves alone again; the months come and go, four whole years; the surviving son looks after his ailing father, the cells that don't want to die; in the end he has to bathe him, feed him

don't worry, says the father, *I'm going to get better*
the spirits are going to operate on me

and the brother who is left doesn't argue with his father's hopes; he doesn't argue with anything, in fact, even if reason—that same reason whose outline he will have to modify—makes him doubt beliefs, doubt faith; he maintains silence and endures, accepts, accompanies; during these years the two men hesitate: what should they celebrate? births, deaths? the first two years, they put an anniversary notice in the paper, then the father's decline accelerates; the life of the remaining brother is a thread strung between day and night; the last winter, he bathes his father, kneeling next to him to help; two mourning figures struggling, whom disease is soon to separate

don't worry, the father says again, *I'm going to get better the spirits are going to operate on me*

but the brother who is left tries to protect himself, interprets events as a necessity of unknown origin whose call and command he feels; then in early summer the father dies, and from that time on it's all a countdown to get out of the Western city and take up life's course again as soon as possible; there's a ceremony, the third one; the family gathers, and friends; but this time, there's no narrative; what's left to say? the father is gone, there's only one left, and he disturbs; the survivors cast around for a *why* when it would be nice if they kept quiet, if they made do with the narratives people devise; but they can't behave any differently; they are alive, their presence troubles; what can they say? the remaining brother now is looking mostly to get away, because he's afraid that if he stays here in this city he'll be carried off; he wants to leave his mother's country, and if he can manage it, the country of his native language; this sentence keeps surfacing in him

to not hear any more . . . to not hear any more about them

and how have these three bodies, that of the brother, the mother, the father, bound themselves together in death? he doesn't want to know; he believes—this is his hope—that he'll be able to start his life again free of the past, that starting from these ruins, in return for the days he's given to his family, he'll be able to resume possession of his life; it takes months, a year, and then another; that ball of anger, of secrets, he thinks he'll be able to leave it behind like a suitcase; his faith in a new life is total; he wants to believe in departure, in the city to the East that he'll be moving to; the brother who is left tells himself that now he's an orphan and that it's from this *orphalineage* that he hopes to invent his *relival*, his return to life; but I've forgotten to say that he boards the train with an archive, three cardboard boxes full of family mementos: letters, emails, manuscripts, childhood photographs; and he crams these bulging boxes into the train compartment where he takes his seat; fleeing, his mind is taken up with his flight; but also with his anger toward those three, his dead; but what he wants, what he is desperately after, is forgetfulness and a blank slate from which to start his life again . . .

and the city in the West is now no longer a habitable place

he leaves his country with his three children

Paris, at his back, is a necropolis

he would like to escape—this is his hope—from the cycle of deaths

he feels that his loved ones have burdened him

with anger

obligations

secrets

in the train that takes him away

the last night train bound to the East

he feels that the fears of several generations

pursue him

he thinks he'll travel faster

than his fears . . .

faster

than the whole past

haunting him

he shuts his sadness away, beside the evidence of his childhood, *in three cardboard boxes*, one for each family member, and the train is traveling, he believes, toward a rediscovery of joy; a free and pioneering time, in a city with no memory; inside him he carries—unknowingly, the idiot—a burnt body that he pushes deep inside his skin; into it he puts, almost unaware, his rage, his survivor's guilt, the voices and gestures of his ghosts, the mother's sad and bitter weight, the father's disappointed faith and hopes of redemption, the brother's indictments; and his childhood is obliterated, he will remember nothing since he knows how it all turned out; he travels eastward to what he believes is a new frontier, forbidden behind the Iron Curtain when he was a child, with a different world on its far side . . .

brothers, toward the sun, toward freedom
brothers toward the light

the train carries him toward what he sees as an adventure, a place where he will find, for himself and his children, another birth; what he is leaving behind is the government of the mother, the father, the brother, the family, the government of his loyalties, his fears, their accusations; for he stands accused, since he survived, since everyone knows he'll be the one to break the order of secrecy someday; and this departure is a flight attempt; he is still young, thirty-five at the time of his flight, three children, and though well aware that these deaths weigh on him, he'll shake free; he pushes everything down into the depths of the body; the fire is one he means to extinguish by forsaking portions of his inner life; he's running away from what's inside him, a burnt landscape where the abandoned hearths of his sufferings will lie in wait for him later; fires that—he'll learn as he falls—will have had the time to gain ground; and what others once believed him to be, a modern young man, will have vanished without a trace; running away, he'll have destroyed himself; and his life will have withdrawn into a sheath of privacy no longer shared with others; in the East, he won't find his life again, only winter mists and shreds of what he would later call *the lineage of men who die . . .*

the lineage of men who die

1937–39

because before the war, his ancestors had been quietly
and secretly reading a buried manuscript, a text
by a forebear whose signature at the end was dated
March 2—this will prove important—1937; the text
will be key in helping the brother who is left, Theseus,
unravel the riddle of his dead kinsmen; right now,
though, he doesn't want to know; doesn't want to
decipher this handwriting from the past that, if he
looked at it, would remind him of his mother's, nor
hear what the voice of his ancestor could teach him; he
is determined, as a *modern*, to look to the future, flee
the past; hear none of what this voice tries to convey:
the memory of a beloved son, the story of a father's
mourning and devotion, at a time when men did not
speak readily of their emotions; it was 1937, two years
before a new war with Germany . . .

. . . and in his train heading East, more than seventy years later, the brother who is left—the fourth generation starting from this forebear—is fleeing the memory of his loved ones, the brother, the mother, the father; he wants to believe in the future, dismisses any call to read what the old man wanted to pass on to his descendants; he found the manuscript one summer, on vacation, in the attic of his grandmother's house but always refused to open it; *the text can wait*, he told himself, and in the train the words of the old man are buried at the bottom of the boxes, with his father's letters, his mother's notebooks, his brother's emails, their childhood photographs; he's leaving, as I've said, to forget; how could he stand to listen to this long-ago grief? how could he accept—having known from a tender age that he would be the *remainer*—the judgments of an old manuscript? as he leaves, Theseus rejects the labyrinth of his genealogy; he believes the son commemorated by his great-grandfather can have nothing to do with his brother's suicide; *ghosts don't exist*, he thinks; he wants each body to have its life, each life its boundaries; that way, so he imagines, he'll be able to resume his own life; *resume his life*, that's why he's on the run, prideful; and though he knows that the present is a book of palimpsests, a seemingly new text on a bed of previously experienced joys and sorrows, he is determined . . .

I won't look back

he thinks

I won't read this old, errant text

J'écris ces courtes notes, désirant recueillir, rassembler, conserver les traits d'une courte existence, ces menus détails, ces mots, ces gestes qui évoquent une figure enfantine. Je voudrais que son souvenir garde les couleurs de la vie. L'infirmité d'une mémoire humaine, même celle d'un père — sinon d'une mère —

"I write these brief notes wanting to collect, gather, and preserve the features of a brief existence; small details, words, and gestures that evoke a childish figure. I would like his memory to retain the colors of life. As human memory is weak, even a father's (though possibly not a mother's), they might otherwise fade away . . .

thus begins his ancestor's text

"Through these memories, which I want to capture before they evaporate, I also hope that Oved's brothers and sisters—*Oved is the son the great-grandfather lost*—and later their children and grandchildren will preserve this family monument and attend to it occasionally.

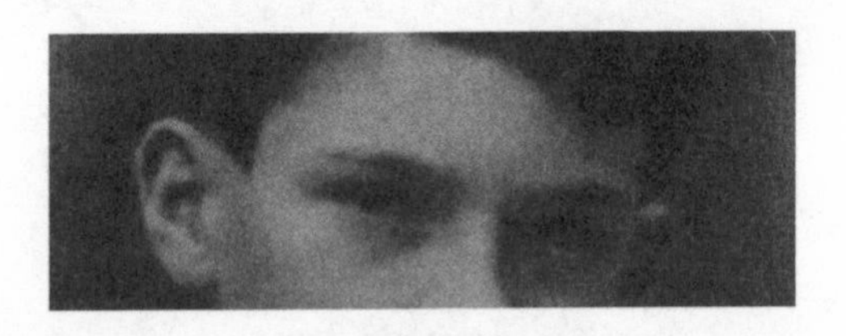

"Oved, *writes the old man*, was born on May 3, 1926. Three years separated him from his brother Nathaniel, and he was followed fourteen months later by his sister, the baby of the family. His name, as often happens, was chosen after long hesitation. We were divided between Elal and Oved. My wife preferred Elal, while I favored Oved. Unsure what to do, I proposed that we give him both names—which we did—and wait to see which he chose. We called him Elal at first, but he gradually became Oved, I don't quite know why. The harmony of these two syllables has since appealed to us. Like his brothers and sisters, he had dark-brown eyes and dark hair. As the family was large and he did not catch our particular attention in infancy, he makes his first appearance in my memory at the age of two. In the summer of 1928 we vacationed on Lake Garda, and friends came to visit. The child enjoyed extraordinary popularity with them. They took it on themselves to photograph him, and though their pictures may be gone, I hope that this fond account by his father will keep these moments vivid. We see Oved perched in a tree, then playing croquet with a mallet that is much too big for him. But he changes, *writes his*

forebear, and here we see him at the end of the 1920s—laughing mischievously under a mop of curly hair—the year that a sculptor, a family friend, carved a bust of him in stone. The sculptor didn't so much copy his model as intuit him, for it wasn't until several months later that he truly started to look like the sculpture. People have said that his face resembled mine; but he had his own look, more elongated, and his eyes were brighter, his features more intense. His reed-like body made him frailer than most of his friends. His gestures were sharp and angular. I noticed that in his sixth year, his physiognomy started to stabilize. From then on, it became ever more defined, until it froze. How elegant he was on his deathbed, and how big he suddenly seemed to me, *the ancestor observes*. Note the oval of his face, the curve of his nostril, the smile that seems to hover on his lips..."

the great-grandfather composed this homage to his son two months after his death; in these lines that look ahead to Oved's passing—the delicate nostrils, the smile at the lips—the whole meaning of this errant and buried text can be read; a text that hovers like the smile at Oved's lips; but the distant descendant of these old sorrows is moving away; Theseus is taking his children to a livable city, as he believes, far from these old memories; he wants nothing to do with these connections woven in the depths of time; the flux coursing through bodies and binding the bones together; life's links to death are invisible to him; and perhaps this corporeal flow that connects bodies will impact him also; only later, when the pieces of the puzzle join together, will he have to accept it . . .

I'll examine the manuscript at some point in the future,
he thinks,
along with the three boxes full of pictures filled
with my family's memory
I'll look at them later, or not

. . . as the train hurtles on, as his children try to find sleep on their stacked bunk beds, he is aiming at a different future; he'd like to erase everything, start over, get away from his dead ones the way you duck out of danger's path; his life is a race to break with attachments, so that his footsteps can proliferate starting from nothing; a *nothing* that—he insists on it—is his home; he throws himself into this life in the East, his only strength an erased memory, and he swears that in spite of everything he'll stay a modern, even if his foundations have crumbled

the city I settle in will be my future

they won't come looking for me there

the *they* being his dead, the brother, the mother, the father, the panoply of their pain, the way his father had of being there by turning away, distancing himself, photographing their youth, their life before, the one that he, the *remainer*, is burying inside himself so deep it will never, he hopes, be unearthed

moving away, he thinks,
I'll manage to forget them; once there I'll live in a different language
stop hearing about them

and one day, in that future, the sound of the new language or the dark of night will close around him; but he is still only starting out: and the other language, the language of the East will, he'd like to believe, help him reinvent himself

I won't need to sing for my children
the lullabies my mother sang to me

"papa est en haut, qui fait des gâteaux, maman est en bas . . ."

I won't need to prolong
the lies that were my hearth and home

besides, even if Theseus tried to connect himself to the past he couldn't; because every reminder of his family is a needle whose sharp stab he avoids; he has to start everything over, life, language, leave his children free to invent; and not repeat anything, not open the black box of time; in him there is a break, a distance, that lets him hope the lineage of men who die will not pursue him

I'll pass the first winters in the Eastern city

they'll ask me what I'm doing there

I won't know what to answer
"warum? warum bist du hier hergezogen?"

what I'm avoiding, that is something I can say
but what I've come to find . . .

Sa curiosité était tournée d'une façon très
particulière du côté de l'Histoire; il avait pour
cette branche de connaissance un don singulier,
que Mlle Rézard sut exploiter et développer.

"His curiosity, *writes the forebear in the hidden manuscript*, was directed quite particularly toward history; he had an unusual gift for this sector of knowledge, which Mademoiselle Rézard was quick to develop. He was entrusted to the care of this woman, who assumed within the household the responsibility for his education. She formed a deep affection toward him. Oved captured her attention, and she set out to cultivate his personality. He adored her. He showed his tenderness toward her in charming ways. How could she not have returned his warm feelings? I have recovered numerous details, *said the ancestor*, thanks to a memorandum that she composed at my request. She writes that our son stood out for his keen desire to learn and his constant eagerness. This sometimes translated into impatience, abrupt gestures, and a rapid flow of speech in which his words bumped up against each other as though there weren't enough time to say everything. Eager for knowledge, Oved was fervent in his work. His teacher never in four years had occasion to reproach him for a missed assignment. I remember that this curiosity, this appetite for knowledge, was mainly apparent in his focused attentiveness. At the dinner table, he passionately followed the discussions I had with his older brothers. Starting at the age of seven, he began inserting himself between me and them; and if my other children laughed, he would reimpose silence. He was inordinately curious, a fact that needs stressing with a child as talented as he, yet it was only with great difficulty that he was able to read and write. At the age of ten, he could still not read fluently. But he excelled at oral work. Oved easily remembered what he was told. He loved being read aloud to, as his schoolmistress often did. But above all, he liked history. I remember that in 1930, a friend, a teacher at the university, gave him a card game in which the point was to match the king, queen, and other royals of various European dynasties: the Bourbon dynasty with its succession of Louis, the Napoleonic line, the Habsburgs . . . The game was a success, and Oved was always in the lead. He developed the idea of starting a collection, and I was enlisted to find cards with the rulers of various kingdoms. He sorted them and mounted them in an album, leaving blank spaces for the missing pieces . . ."

. . . years later, reading his ancestor's manuscript, the brother who was left made a note of Oved's passion for family lines, genealogy, and *missing pieces*; but for the moment, in the train taking him far from the Western city and the memory of his loved ones, he refuses to listen to any of this; I think this refusal corresponds to what he has up till now seen as his strength: dodging; the idiot naively thinks that leaving his country and dropping his language will be enough; he naively thinks that as a modern, it's possible to *break off*, to *find freedom* . . .

not to see the hanged brother when he closes his eyes

not to have the indictment of his mother, her violence encroach on his future

not to have the hate he has harbored keep him from loving

because he also knows that in some cultures, the names of children are changed so death won't find them, and as he leaves, he too believes this; he thinks he'll shake off his family by erasing his footsteps, changing his name; and maybe too, in the train, running away from his forebear's narrative, he's afraid of what Oved's story will tell him: the paradox of this thirst, this quest for continuity, on the part of the very person who broke it down . . .

a story of impossible attachment

a sundered genealogy, where the one who is fragile hides behind a story of strength

Theseus is a descendant of this line of omissions and deaths, but he wants to be free; he sees himself, idiotically, as a person who sets off for distant lands to change his life; in the train, he tries to imagine what awaits him; what it will be like, tomorrow, in the country of the other language; I know that later on he will come to understand what he came to the Eastern city seeking; but for the moment, I'll leave him to his illusions; he is running from the labyrinth, looking at the flashes of light hitting the train windows, slicing through the dark...

this city, he thinks, *is the place I have chosen*

to start my life over

to deflect the lineage of men who die

to escape their hold

but he goes about it so lamely, poor guy; he thinks memory can be erased; while Oved was fascinated by lineage, Theseus insists that you can thrive in an orphanage; the errant text will be a discovery for him when he falls, when everything in him collapses; when he becomes aware that Oved, the beloved child, was obsessed by dynasties; it will be a shock to him, the *remainer*; to feel in the collapse of his bones, his kidneys, his teeth, that this is what he is: a brother attached to the brother, tied to a history of suffering and loss; and this train, though he knows where it's going, though he thinks he knows, isn't it carrying him, in the end, toward the past rather than the future?

Il connaissait tous ces personnages comme
on connaît des vivants : il savait comment
ils étaient faits, comment ils s'habillaient,
quelles étaient leurs relations de famille.
Feuilletant un jour avec moi un livre qui
reproduit des œuvres de primitifs français, il
identifia sans erreur et sans hésitation
— bien qu'il n'y eut aucun texte visible —
les portraits royaux, que ce fusse celui de
François I, de Charles VII, ou de Jean le
Bon.

"He knew all these historical figures, *writes the ancestor about his son Oved*, the way you might know living beings; he knew what they looked like, how they dressed, what their family relationships were. One day, paging through a book of early French painters with me, he correctly and unhesitatingly identified—though no text was visible—the royal portraits: they included Francis I, Charles VII, and John the Good. Oved knew that the Capetian and Valois dynasties had died out. He kept perfect track of the daughters of Louis XV, the brothers of Napoleon Bonaparte, and the various descendants of Louis Philippe. He could draw all kinds of dynastic charts, charts that we discovered in his papers. One day, in response to his curiosity, a friend gave him a genealogical tree of the Habsburgs. Oved learned it by heart. He knew the dates, the names, and the locations of battles. I sometimes amused myself by exhibiting his talents. I did this once with a man named Zimmerman, a professor of geography and an amateur historian, who joined me in asking Oved questions. I had my son recite the succession of Austrian emperors. That's very good, said Zimmerman, but do you know the kings of France and their dates? No, said Oved, I'm just learning them. Well, said Zimmerman, I do, and he started to recite them. When he reached Philip I, he hesitated: 1060 to 1105 . . . It's 1108! Oved interrupted. Zimmerman burst out laughing, but he agreed. Oved, *wrote the ancestor*, would thumb through the dictionary even before he knew how to read, and he could find his way to the pages where there were portraits of kings or paintings of historic scenes. Lying on the rug with the book open before him, he would spend hours at this game. Later, he would find other sources of information in my library. He particularly liked a manual called *A Methodical and Comparative History of Europe, with Synoptic Tables and Engraved Illustrations.* This work, which dated to the post-Napoleonic Restoration—although my own copy, *the ancestor notes*, is a later reprint—served to educate the duc de Bordeaux and the princes of Naples and Tuscany. The book divides history into separate reigns. Each table is accompanied by an engraved illustration and a list of events—laws, inventions, public works projects. So much to gratify our little Oved! In 1933, he was also given an illustrated *History of France* and a book on the major battlefields, along with a number of books I'd received in childhood but never read. Oved would open them on his bed in the morning to peruse them earnestly. His collection also contained books for young readers on Caesar, Henry IV, and Richard the Lionheart. What was remarkable in one so young was the fine-grained detail of his knowledge. When Oved knew a thing, his certainty was unassailable. I challenged him any number of times for the pure fun of it. But *Papa*, he would say, I'm sure . . ."

. . . in the years following his older brother's death and during the time it took him to get used to the East—and, as I'd be tempted to put it, *settle into exile, make his nest*—the surviving brother, Theseus, did not read his ancestor's manuscript; he was too busy mourning his loved ones, or rather, erasing their memory; his hope was to start over entirely, and this hope flickered in him; he wanted to come out on top, to do what others, his role models, had done: men and women who had succeeded in establishing themselves in another language; *winners who had broken cleanly, severed with their genealogy*; on spring evenings, sitting on the balcony of his apartment, he would someday experience joy; he would say: *I, too, have succeeded*; and in the sunlight he would watch his children play in the park before his house, and he'd bask in the pleasure of forgetting

I'll get free of this family, this history

he thinks

after all the deaths, all the lies
I'll build another home

this was the hope that nourished him; and in those moments of happiness—for darkness is stubborn—he would remember a phrase that had always struck him as extraordinarily false, that *everything is for the best in the best of all possible worlds*; Theseus can't be sure that his future in the East will allow his scars to heal, but his children are what help him keep fighting; by leaving, he thinks, *I am taking them away from the curse and from the city in the West*, from its gray roofs and society intrigues; and, on the train, when his children finally go to sleep, he thinks at least I'll have done that, moved them away from the past . . .

I'll have to learn to live, to breathe
in the language of the East

and if I don't manage, I can always focus on
the sight of my children launching themselves in time

and he thinks

no, I won't read the errant manuscript

J'ai déjà dit son goût pour les tableaux
synoptiques, avec force colonnes et accolades. Il
en confectionnait de toutes sortes, pour son
travail et pour son plaisir. Il classait ses papiers.
avec des satisfactions de précoce archiviste. Le
rangement de son bureau était une grande joie.

"I've already mentioned his love of synoptic tables, *writes the forefather*, with multiple columns and brackets. He cooked up all sorts, both for his schoolwork and for pleasure. He filed his papers with the gusto of a precocious archivist. Neatening his desk was a source of joy. One day, he must have been nine years old at the time, I showed him an engraved portrait of the duc d'Aumale and asked if he knew who it was. It's Louis Philippe's next to last son, said Oved. And what did he do? I asked. He took part in the campaign to colonize Algeria. That's right, I said. But I think you're wrong in one thing, the duc d'Aumale is Louis Philippe's youngest son. No, *Papa*, said Oved. His youngest is the duc de Montpensier. And he was right. Another day, I remember, he was examining a portrait bust in the scullery. I proposed that he should have it: if you like it, you're welcome to it; it's Napoleon. Oved said: That's not Napoleon, *Papa*, that's Bonaparte! Napoleon never dressed that way once he'd become emperor . . . Such was this boy's curious gift for family lines and genealogies, *notes the ancestor*. Oved wanted things to be arranged in a very orderly way. He couldn't stand for his drawers to be disorganized. His dream was to have his own room because his brother's messiness, though slight, distressed him. It was his habit to lay out his brother's clothes for him in the morning, to keep the cupboard they shared from disarray. Oved had difficulty reading, as I've said, but he was good at geography. He enjoyed drawing maps, and he took great pleasure in arithmetic, which he considered a game. If anyone expressed surprise that he came up so quickly with a result, he would laugh: I have a trick, he would say, but I don't want to tell it. His virtuosity at counting was precocious, already apparent when he was five. I remember, *the ancestor writes*, how easily he would leapfrog by sevens up to one hundred, and his ability to solve a problem that many find surprisingly hard: what is one million minus one? It's true that he worked slowly. In sixth grade, his results were disastrous. In French, he was ranked twenty-second. In arithmetic, fifteenth out of twenty-eight. In Latin, thirteenth out of twenty-nine. In English, twenty-sixth. But in history he was first in his class . . .

The ancestor quotes a letter of Oved's

Tel them that I canot rite them
each seperately because it wood use up

all my leter paper, but in the mean time
wish them all a good weak

then he observes

"I've seen children with spelling problems, but they didn't have Oved's extraordinary memory. Was it because he had such difficulty learning to read or because his intelligence was basically oral? Whatever the case, Oved was passionate about everything that he undertook. His taste for history was not just an offshoot of his curiosity, or a mental game, or a thirst for knowledge, *the forebear continues, finding a place in his text for every aspect of his son's temperament that was singular or different*. To give a sense of Oved's intensity, I will just cite some of his childhood sayings that struck us. One day in September 1933, when he was six, one of his sisters jokingly asked him a silly question: Whom do you love more, *Papa* or *Maman*? He answered with a certain degree of heat: *Papa!* Another time, his tutor said to him: When you're eighteen, you'll have to ask your father to take you on a trip. Oh! What a nice idea! said Oved. And where would you like to go? the woman asked. Would you like to travel around the world? Oved was practically offended: The world doesn't interest me, he said. I want to see France! It was touching, *Theseus's great-grandfather comments*, to see in this delicate boy such a robust attachment to the country that had taken us in. Oved, *he added*, had made French history his religion. He was in awe of the royals, but he was every bit as approving of the French Revolution. I would read him passages from Michelet's history, and his imagination was fired by the continuity between the ancien régime and the Republic. I remember that it had been a painful realization for him that he could never be king. From his earliest years, Oved had never imagined anything for himself but to rule and govern France . . ."

. . . at the point when Theseus was leaving for the East, reading his ancestor's text could surely have helped him; it strikes me today that it might have given him the key to understanding the turn his life had taken: the act of breaking with his country, his family, and his whole past seems to take an opposite direction from the track laid down by the little ghost: reading the errant text, he might have woven the kind of ties that develop through the looking glass between a reflection and the person observing himself: the inversion that occurs when left becomes right and right becomes left, where the identical face appears, but flipped; his departure, his break for the hills, his intent on erasure, might possibly have struck him as a negative of Oved's passion for the fables of French continuity; his quest to break off, to disrupt genealogy, and the impossibility he felt of *being French*, were these an echo of what Oved wanted, the child who died so long ago, who would have liked to be king?

what can I possibly expect from my lineage?
have I not lost my family?

Can Theseus want anything other
than to forget his loved ones?

I have never belonged

he thinks

I'm not my parents' son

the day of my birth still lies ahead

. . . setting off to the East, Theseus could have resolved
the enigma of his brother's death; if only he had
read the manuscript; but he'll have to wait for light
to reveal the secret links between generations;
tomorrow, at the foot of his building, there will be
an ice cream vendor and, on the other side of the
street, under the lindens, a park; and a language that
he'll want to learn but that will rebuff him; I can't
say when things will start to change, but it won't be
before the fourth or fifth autumn; for now he takes off
with his children aboard a train that is carrying him,
as he believes, toward a reinvention of himself; he
has shoved the three cardboard boxes and the errant
manuscript under the lower bunks: a carton for the
brother, the mother, and the father; it will all wait,
he won't reread anything, he won't relate; years later,
though, when everything starts to fall, he'll have to
start listening to what's been brewing under his skin,
in his bones, where his memories with his brother
are buried, the laughter he shared with his father, the
moments of tenderness with his mother; but for now,
nothing, he doesn't want to hear it, and here's how we

should picture the idiot escaping toward the city in the East: his childhood days are stagnant inside him, he pretends to be alive, and he rides triumphantly ahead of time . . .

Nous avions souvent parlé de le mener à Paris. Ce
projet avait été remis à l'été prochain à l'occasion
de l'Exposition de 1937. Que de regrets aujourd'hui,
de ne pas lui avoir donné cette joie! Car il s'était
déjà préparé à ce voyage. Il savait tout ce qu'il
voulait voir à Paris, les grands monuments de notre
histoire: Notre Dame, le Louvre, la Conciergerie,
le Tombeau des Invalides, celui de l'Arc de Triomphe.

"We had often talked of taking him to Paris, *the ancestor writes of his son in the manuscript that Theseus still refused to read*, but the project was deferred until the summer to coincide with the International Exposition of 1937. That we never managed to offer him that pleasure has been a source of regret ever since. For he'd prepared himself for the visit. He knew of everything there was to see in Paris; Notre Dame, the Louvre, the Conciergerie, the tombs at Les Invalides, the grave of the unknown soldier at the Arc de Triomphe. His eagerness comes through in a letter he wrote his brother in October, after his brother set off to boarding school, leaving him alone at home.

the ancestor quotes

Your incredably lucky to spend time in Paris.
When you anser my letter, please let me kno
what your doing and how is the sity,
let me kno!

"Oved, *he continues*, was a child who wrote execrably, despite his prodigious gift of memory. And how can I forget the moment when, on his last night, at a point when he had already stopped talking and a nurse had taken up her station at the foot of his bed, he suddenly sat up, wanting to pray? But the poor child didn't know the words. The boy wanted to pray, but the words to the prayer escaped him, they were gone. And I asked myself, *writes the ancestor*, was it a consequence of our assimilation into French life? Alas, we no longer know, we have forgotten how to pray. In his final moments, Oved tried, but no words appeared in the place where he searched for them. He knew all the kings of all the dynasties of Europe, the dates of every French ruler, but he had lost the words of the prayer. Our assimilation had happened so quickly. And there, at the heart of words, at the heart of France, whose king he dreamed of becoming—a Jewish king for France!—*the ancestor stresses*, in place of God there was nothing but a blank; nothing to implore, nothing to greet him or offer refuge; and to my great shame, *says the ancestor*, I was unable to help him. The secular believe, *he observes*, that we can live without the prayers that have connected us for centuries to what is greater than ourselves; but what can a child of eleven hold on to when he dies? What is left to him if we insist that he should be just an assimilated French citizen? Oddly enough, *the ancestor comments*, as I review the memory of these extraordinarily painful moments, it calls to mind an entirely different passion: Oved's passion for play. The intensity he wanted to put into his prayer, that prayer devoid of words, *the ancestor notes*, may be the same intensity that I saw him pour into his games as a child. I remember that Oved loved riding his bicycle. I can still see him turning and turning on the garden paths behind our house. Was this already a prayer? Childhood joy, the passion for play? He had an even greater love of swimming, which he learned to do in a small pool. I can see him splashing out into the water, then leaping in all at once. Later he threw himself into soccer, and he dreamed of learning to ski. He gave it a try on a trip to the mountains during what would be his last winter. In the last letter he wrote, he asks for a little money to spend on the 'cherlift'...

Papa, *the ancestor quotes*, send me a little mony for the cherlift.

"I wouldn't want my portrait of Oved to show him as too perfect. He was an affectionate child, but he could also be violent. When angry, he would use his fists, and his fits of nerves could be explosive. He was often jealous, and he hated for anyone else to sit on my knees. As he told his brothers and sisters:

I don't want you to give *Papa* a kiss.

"Oved enjoyed the first months of his sixth-grade year a great deal. At the end of November, we thought he looked pale and decided to extend his vacation somewhat. On December 13, he set off for a youth camp in the mountains run by a nurse. For our part, we'd arranged to spend time in the Val d'Aosta with friends. We had decided against bringing Oved for fear that he would tire himself out trying to keep up with the older set. He let us know he was sorry not to be included, but he seemed happy enough those first days at camp, and his letters telegraphed nothing but joyous excitement. We came home on a Thursday morning, December 31. Oved was supposed to return the same day to have New Year's dinner with us. Shortly after we arrived back, we received a telephone call from his youth camp. It was the directress asking us to send a car for Oved. We learned that two days earlier he had had a bout of fever. The doctor had been to see him, we were told, and *everything was fine*. The woman added that it was only out of caution that she recommended he return home by car rather than take the late train.

Talmaï, the predecessor, then starts in
on the final pages of his homage

he narrates the last hours of Oved's life

the child who wanted to be the first Jewish king of France

"The day went by, *he writes*, in the warm afterglow of our successful vacation. The friends we'd brought along on our jaunt had showered us, on the threshold of 1937, with candies. We talked a bit about Germany and what was happening there. What a good idea it had been, I said, to move to France! What a trial it must be to hear this strident chancellor constantly calling into question every element of the fragile equilibrium that holds European peace together! But at eight o'clock Oved arrived, and the ambience rose to a scream. The child had been returned to us, but in a daze. He could barely speak or stand on his feet. We brought him upstairs and sat him on his bed. His brothers and sisters gathered around, but he didn't respond to them. His mother undressed him: Leave us! she said. A rash covered Oved's body, *the ancestor notes*, and there were white spots on his throat. We took his temperature: 104 degrees. The doctor was summoned. After auscultating the patient, he announced that there was nothing to worry about, that everything would be fine. He left us saying he would return on January 2, and, quietly alarmed, we busied ourselves organizing Oved's care. The child was isolated: no one was to enter his room without first putting on a clean smock; for this reason, until I thought the following day to wrap myself in my bathrobe, I stayed away from him during those last, darkest hours.

here Talmaï switches into the present tense
as though time were starting to tremble

"The night goes well enough, *he writes*. Oved recovers from the strain of traveling and the car ride back from the mountains. He says very little; his mother, wanting to husband his strength, asks him hardly any questions. She gleans a few brief clues. Two days earlier, in the youth camp where we had sent him to rest—what a horrible notion this 'rest' now seems, *Theseus's great-grandfather observes*, he was put in isolation; he spent the night alone. He says that on that morning, which was Tuesday, he had gone skating and caught cold. In the evening, waking from sleep, he reaches out with his little hand and turns to face me . . .

Papa, we can't go when we choose

he says, and also

what's going to happen to me
if I don't know the prayers?

and the ancestor answers

you're not going to die, Oved

you're a king, and kings don't die

and Oved says again

Papa, we can't go when we choose

then

"On the morning of January 1, *writes the great-grandfather, whom we sense to be trembling more than ever,* we go in search of a sick-nurse; I am lucky enough to find a friend who has already cared for several family members. Knowing her to be gentle and firm, I am convinced of a good outcome. Yet hardly does she approach our patient than she says something that worries me

"At noon, the child's condition is in stasis. His fever is running high. That afternoon I bring the brothers and sisters for a few visits. When I come back, toward four or five p.m., his heart is weakening. We call the doctor urgently. On seeing Oved, he agrees with us. He calls for a second opinion. We reach out to the doctor's colleague and manage to contact him. He would reach the patient's bedside at eight o'clock. That night, the two doctors draw up the battle plan. There are to be baths, injections. I walk them out to their car, and on my return the nurse is distraught. We now embark on the hours of this one night, so short and so atrociously long, when without having had the time to fight, we are forced into the realization that all is lost. We must accept this and also resist it.

Talmaï writes these words that read
like cries addressed to a desperately empty sky

God's will! The way of the world!
We ourselves are powerless!

"Toward four a.m., the doctor returns. He can't think what else to try, but he believes Oved may yet come through. I go to wake Oved's brothers and sisters, hoping that together we will be able to help him. But he dies at eight o'clock on January 2.

the old man says

he is now a perfect soul

as though perfection on its own
could take the dead child's place

"And he is also there, *he continues*, on his bed. His furrowed features are once again calm. A smile has returned to his lips.

How beautiful is the child that God has taken

he adds, finding more words intended to console
though for the brother who is left they provoke an anger
he will finally have to acknowledge

"I remain at his bedside, *the ancestor writes*. And all that he's been, with his elegance, his delicacy, his vivacity, his passion, fills me with emotion. All that he was to me, all that I guessed he might be—it all has no more substance than a dream. Yet I would like this dream to last. The death of a child is affliction in its purest form. But this affliction must not be allowed to dissipate.

"After his death we cannot remain unchanged, and we must be guided by Oved; his death will weave a stronger bond around us. I wanted him, *he writes*, to spend his final days in our house. At the same time I know that one day the house will again be filled with laughter and dancing. On that day, his shadow will hover over us

then Talmaï the forebear's last lines,

like an invitation to return to life, issued on March 2, 1937, the day the manuscript was finished

words that the old man offered his descendants by way of encouragement

"We have an obligation to perform our duties, *he writes*, and history must not come to an end. My children, brothers and sisters of our Oved, I promise you that I won't shut myself away with him in a crypt. I want to see you grow up. Come, children, let us gather him in our arms, let us carry him together through the good and bad days on the path that still lies ahead for us, and let us pronounce in his name the words of the forgotten prayer, that his soul may enlighten us; let us turn toward the heavenly land that is our refuge in grief; let us find strength in all that he has given us and walk forward."

. . . thus ends the errant text that passed from hand to hand, from generation to generation, secretly, silently, before coming to Theseus seventy years later; a manuscript to the memory of Oved, the child who dreamed of becoming the *first Jewish king of France*; Theseus falling, falling in the city to the East and finally reading these secret sentences, would underline these words

children, brothers and sisters of our Oved, I promise you
that I won't shut myself away with him in a crypt
I want to see you grow up

come, children,
let us gather him in our arms, let us carry him together
through the good and bad days on the path that still lies
ahead for us . . .

Theseus would see it as a long Kaddish spoken for the women and men of the future, saying

may there be abundant peace from heaven
and a new life, and comfort and salvation
in the world which will be renewed . . .

but when he comes to it, months and years after his escape in a train carrying him eastward, he can only read it, this errant manuscript, this Kaddish of hope and grief, in the light of all that has happened: the death of his brother, his mother, his father, and what he will have learned of his great-grandfather's death . . .

for on November 30, 1939,
a few months after war was declared

having lost all hope of seeing peace return to Europe

having seen his sons, Oved's older brothers,
set off for war as he had seen,
a few years earlier, his brother
set off for another war

old Talmaï, "he who hides," shut himself
in his office
and with his service pistol
put a bullet through his head

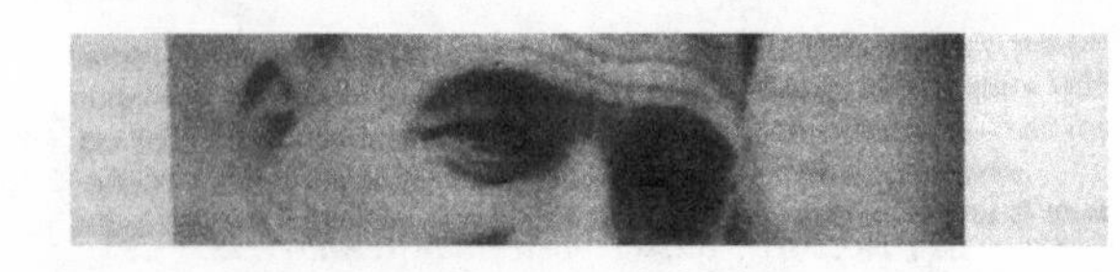

and his affirming words, the life impulse he had worked to pass on, became a dead letter; he had imagined that, once the mourning was over, his family would "laugh" and "dance," but instead he had cast over it the shameful veil of his suicide; the pistol shot was hushed up, swept away in the chaos of the general mobilization; Talmaï's body fell and was covered by all the other men and women who died in the war, or who disappeared or were deported or exterminated; but was it a father's grief at the death of his child, or his memory of the battles of the last Great War, or the all-too-forgotten Jewish prayer and the imminent ruin of his love for France that led to his taking his own life? was it the fear of losing his other children in the battles that lay ahead?

on his train journey, Theseus might already understand, if he'd read the manuscript, that it all started there, with this gesture of despair, *the lineage of men who die*; if he had not been so afraid of the echoes of the past that ricochet from age to age at matter's core, he could have looked back; but because he is a modern, because he hopes to break with this cycle of the dead and leave the twentieth century, he looks obstinately to the future; and in the train's glass window, he sees the reflection of his sleeping children; he tells himself that by leaving he is tearing them away from a dark mechanism, and the lights of the outside world are flashing over their faces . . .

I won't do what Talmaï did, he swears to himself, *I won't do what my brother, Jerome, did, I won't give up; I'll break with my lineage; I won't be king, I'll forget my own name, I'll forget my language; I won't do what they did, I won't commit suicide; I won't let the past haunt the future, death contaminate life; I'll invest myself in the novelty of the Eastern city, the forward thrust of my children in time; besides, what connection have I to these men who kill themselves, and what hold has sorrow over me? nothing can touch me, I'm young and don't want to die; I'm setting off toward the heart of the old charnel house to build a new life; I leave behind the Western city that my brother would have liked to leave behind for the lakes, the mountains, and snow-covered peaks; I go toward a new drive and a new energy; I'll offer myself to the north wind, to the hollow plain that is soon to be swallowed by water; I want to see what the severed city looks like; see what scar tissue is forming at the site of ancient wounds; I'm leaving for a country where no one knows my name; to put an ocean of land between me and my lineage; I'll change my name if I have to, I'll change languages . . .*

yesterday,
I reopened boxes
full of images

BERLIN, 2017

. . . but Theseus failed, he didn't manage to erase everything, and the shadows of his loved ones followed him to the Eastern city; despite interposing a language, borders, rivers between himself and his life before, none of it worked; five years have passed since his departure on the night train, his vow; five years since he left the adored country of young Oved: that proud old land at the end of the continent where they call themselves *French*; he also tracks the thirteen years since the death of Jerome, his brother, who dreamed of mountains and wide horizons; thirteen years of trying to forget and break with his loved ones; and now he jots down these lines to mark what is collapsing in him . . .

now that a veil of night has fallen over the city where I went to rebuild myself, far from the memory of my loved ones, from the season of deaths that carried them off, I've come to understand that I will not succeed; in thirteen years of avoidance, I tried to delete all trace of them but failed; my brother's hanging is still there between me and the passing days, and I'm falling; the city I fled to offers me no respite; it's an open-air cemetery haunted by last century's ghosts; signs of their passage hail me at every intersection; on the paving, when I leave the house, the Stolpersteine *gleam in the December rain; I read the names on the little cobblestones of memory, and these names meld with the names of Oved and my great-grandfather; of those who followed them, deported during the war, the sons, uncles, cousins; those who would fall in the second half of the century slipping in the shower—their own shower—or who, like my brother, knotting their neck to a rope, to a gas pipe, would die in the wake of a history that goes on and on . . . the past persists a long time, it contaminates by slow increments and keeps on killing after the immediate cause is gone; but who will gauge this long-term damage? the Eastern city oppresses me now; I'm surrounded by History, when I thought to escape it; vast stretches of fear awake in me; the left side of my body—my brother was left-handed—has seized up; my teeth are infected, my back is giving out; everything is crumbling, and all around me I feel the darkness that I want to emerge from, but the path I've chosen won't allow it; I can find no support in the future and nothing in the past to hold on to; and I sense that I will have to cross this darkness, try to see in this night of time, connect the memories to each other, and my brother to this secret text that celebrates Oved, the son who wanted to be king; I will have to join lives together across epochs to heal the dead and, counter to the direction of my flight, reconnect with them; understand how ghosts impinge on the living; because I finally have to accept this verdict: there is something vaster than conscious memory; there is the deep memory anchored in the body's matter*

... and so the brother who is left decides to open the boxes; he tells himself that maybe it's time to turn back, and he has no choice anyway; the doctors he consults so as to stop his fall can't find anything; why the pain in his temples, the inflammation at the roots of his teeth, in the bones in his back? why is his body racked, thirteen years after his brother's death? thirteen years and everything is falling apart, no one can help him; he'd like for life to be simple, for mourning to occur during the period of mourning, for the body to be a body that moderns can deal with; he would like to leave it all behind and go on as before; *as before*, to sever, break with, and continue stubbornly disparaging genealogy, kings, and all nations; to get through this, Theseus would be willing even to say a prayer, if prayers were heard

why does my beloved, my King, hide?
I let fall the supplication from my lips
no one answers

I ask about my dream in the night
no one explains

I tell myself then that I won't make it
because life is sealed shut

. . . but nothing is of any use, and his body slips away; Theseus is at wit's end, not knowing where to turn; he imagines that pills—anti-inflammatories—will free him from his pain, and it will all be fine; he can continue to live as a modern, to move forward, to veil history in oblivion; but there is no drug, no surgery, for what is wrong with him, no *course of treatment*; the scans, the MRIs, show nothing; the doctors, men of reason, talk of "psychosomatics," as though the problem lurked in his soul; yet the collapse is real; it's physical, it's crushing him; he'd like to stay within the bounds of what is *scientifically* demonstrable; find a doctor who will free him from the burden of being a survivor; for the moment he's staying away from other, wilder treatments; later, I know, people will counsel him to return to God; a woman healer will bind him with tefillin, even his heart, and talk to him of previous lives; there will be shamans, meditators; sages and Chinese reflexologists, who will tell him to clap his hands so the vibrations can expel the toxins; his quest for new life will bring him in contact with people who talk of *fasciae*, who initiate him into the art of letting go, who teach him to communicate with *the body's water* to cleanse his wounds; there will be those who introduce him to the work of Moreno on psychodrama and group therapy; but for the moment, he just doesn't know; he senses that within him is *a genealogical fear* that's carrying him off, and the threat that families use to intimidate those who *might* reveal their secret; those who, often to their detriment, are the guardians of order; and also the dead, who form a stern, silent conclave that unnerves him; but he doesn't see this conclave; he avoids looking at it squarely, tries to find a way around what happened; and up till now he considered this pocket of denial his raison d'être; the brother who is left is still refusing, but he's starting to feel he has no choice; he is going to have to *face up to the facts*, open the boxes he brought with him; because you need something to hold on to, or else life goes into free fall, and maybe memory is the anchor that he needs? that is his hope when he dumps the boxes out on the floor: Talmaï's manuscript, the photographs, the childhood photo albums, the whole of Jewish life hidden from view on German soil . . .

Theseus writes

I don't see anything for the moment, it's all just a haze of anger and regret; leaving my country, boarding the train to the East, I knew that the errant text was deep in those boxes with other documents, with letters of my mother's, my brother's, my father's; but the flood of memory that washes through people's bodies from life to life is so opaque, so unnoticed, that the interplay between the traumas of the past and the present is beyond me; I see nothing, understand nothing; one has to take oneself out of the picture—die, kill the observer—to get close to matter's secret; and now I'm on my hands and knees; what was buried in my boxes forms the carpet of memories on which I must learn to walk again, but I'm still crawling; and it's all a confusion of forgotten faces; I see myself in these photographs, but it isn't me; I see bits of a childhood, but it isn't my childhood; I see my brother, but he isn't my brother anymore; this spilled-out archive could belong to a stranger; I am not he, I think, this is not where I come from, not who I have ties with; I don't belong to this era; it's all been severed; I managed to break with the fear that the ancestor drilled into the bodies of the descendants, but...

Theseus is looking for a way out of the labyrinth, he wants to avoid the monster; confronted with the many images spread at his feet, he'd like to return to life without even looking at them; and though he gives people the impression of still being alive, everything inside him is actually in shreds, his back, the roots of his teeth, everything is dying; the brother who is left is rotting in place; he made the mistake of thinking that the members of his family were *outside*, in the coffins where he left them, at the bottom of a distant crypt in a sloping cemetery on a lake ringed with mountains near the Swiss border, when they are in fact here, in his body water, his bones; and it's at this moment that the city in the East withdraws into the endless night of winter, offers up its deserted sidewalks to the frigid winds; he can't forget any longer, in pain he understands it; one by one he picks up the photographs, there are hundreds of them and it's more than he can do, he doesn't have the strength; but his eyes, his eyes manage to turn to the signs on the ground; they try to recognize the people there, and yet what he finds each time is a block of once-flaming matter that has cooled, and from which he's trying to shake free...

they say that survivors flee
to get away from the memories haunting them

but years later they find themselves beset
with mysterious pathologies: an aphasia, a paralyzed hand,
a shoulder that stiffens up

this has been studied in "psychogenealogy"

the aphasia related to a word one wants to say
but can't manage to pronounce

the sudden paralysis:
the trace left by a loved hand in one's own

that shoulder: metabolized from something shouted
during an emergency:

"Lift him onto your shoulders!"

we are woven of words, the body is an envelope
in which everything intermingles: the word and the
chemistry of our water, tissue,
nerves, bones . . .

but who can know the circuits of this intermingling?

matter, language

who has penetrated the secret of this inscription

when the body's chemistry becomes language
and language tries desperately to name
the incomprehensible chemistry of
human matter?

that's what is happening to him, what his body is doing

he no longer manages to carry everything he has contained

and Theseus fortunately has several weeks of solitude ahead of him; his children stay mostly with their mother; and how could he take care of them in this state? the smallest gesture, the tiniest task, tortures him; he can no longer carry anything, not even his own weight; prone, he contemplates the spilled-out evidence of his childhood, of the family he sought to erase by moving East; everything he thought he could annihilate by going away, by changing his name and his language, is there: images that, he hopes, will bring down the wall he has erected between himself and the past: the ancestor's memories, the voices of his brother, his mother, his father . . . the ghost of Oved, the child who wanted to be the *first Jewish king of France*; during the thirteen years of his flight—I'm tempted to write, of his *attempted escape*—he has repeated a kind of mantra under his breath . . .

I want to destroy the past

EVERYTHING

erase those who lived inside those names
the known, familiar names . . .

Talmaï, the ancestor

Oved and Nathaniel, his two sons

Esther, daughter of Nathaniel, and Gatsby, as my father was called,

names

my sonic envelope, my house

I want to be able to say:

I have no brother, no mother, no father, no origin

I am moving to the East

because

I want to find the present again

and go toward the future

. . . and this mantra about erasure carried Theseus to the East; he would come back to life armed with the energy he drew from fleeing; but having cut himself off from so much, he finds himself inhabiting a nowhere land; and now his body is falling and forcing him to turn back, to look into all that he had rejected: *genealogy, lineage, the lie of childhood, the mother's dreams, the father's illusions, the myths and stories told by the descendants of the ancestor who shot himself with a pistol, though no one was allowed to mention it; then the prosperous history of the* Trente Glorieuses, *which should have allowed everything to be rebuilt*... this is the point Theseus has reached when he surrenders to the forces killing him; he can see a patch of sky above the walls of his maze; the images on the carpet at his feet are the walls within which he must learn to walk again in order to find, as he hopes, joy, his memories of his brother, the smells of the fireplace

when we burned sugar cubes on the coals
before pouring them into a bowl of milk...

for these were the treasures of his childhood: no continuity, but bits, flashes, spurts, as when they went to gather chestnuts, and the tireless mother, Esther, found the time to pick flowers, but all that was long ago

and I have forgotten it

. . . with the images around me, I start to take mechanical note of what I see: faces, moments when the faces light up on a seaside vacation or in the mountains in winter, where bodies struggle along snowy trails; looking at the pictures, I try to feel the extent to which these scenes relate or don't relate to emotions I could say are attached to my memories; in these imprints of time, I have difficulty recognizing my brother: how can I be sure it's him, if I relate to the scene only through photographs?

this was your life

say the images, some in color, some in black and white; speaking in English, a language that offered me an out from my own—is this the reason for my many flights, to emerge from the folds of a language *so as to stop hearing . . . stop hearing about them . . .* ? what we call *preuves* in French, in English is called *evidence*; in the singular form, it's *a piece of evidence*, as though evidence were a block; the boxes contain this "evidence," which I should be able to integrate *as a block* but manage to see only bit by bit—*piece by piece, image after image . . .*

this is your childhood

each of the images seems to say, as though arm wrestling with my mind; seeing them, I realize how separated I've become from the joy, the happiness I shared with my brother; where has our laughter gone? I slowly become aware of what, till then, I had managed to do best in my escape to the East: this act of dissimulation through which I denied the evidence of my life; instead of a new life, I've thrown myself into an exitless well; wanting to erase the memory of my dead brother, I've allowed all the other scenes of my life to be swept away, and now I need to start right here, with the brother who hangs his neck

from a gas pipe

to interpret

"a gas pipe"

and Jerome, my brother, why was that name given you?

JEROME

this first name, what does it know, what does it carry?

body I grew up with, voice that spoke my name

you who lived inside the name Jerome

a name harking back to the life of a saint whose task
was to translate ancient Hebrew texts on the origin of the
world

"Jerome of Stridon"

who was painted by Caravaggio and many other masters

who had to aggregate diverse scripts, many deriving
from Greek, Hebrew, Aramaic
and cobble the diverse myths into a single heritage

Jerome, my brother,
we live in stories that overpower us
but why kill yourself?

what couldn't you translate?

as your survivor, must I see your death
as an indictment of all history?

right now, it's all a jumble and I can't see anything, understand anything; I just need to pick up the thread and remove this rope that, after taking you away, has quietly knotted itself around my neck; because the brother is the brother, and it only takes one missing link for everything to start falling: the active self, the capacity to say *I*, one's vitality, strength, ability to love; *it only takes one missing link*, and this thing that destabilizes me, this link of the brother who is missing, you, the witness of my earliest years, who taught me to play, I wanted to erase you and prove that *I* can stand alone; but my body tells me that the flight is coming to an end; I'm falling, and innumerable ailments beset me: paralysis of the left side of my body, infection at the roots of my teeth, and inflammation in my back the whole length of the dura mater to the sacrum, which no doctor can explain; shipwrecked, here in the East, I repeat a promise to myself . . .

not to do as you did, Jerome,

to go through the old prayers, across the genealogical breaks

believe at least in my task

clean the dark waters of time

escape the labyrinth

restore the missing name and the absent prayer

never again dream of suturing the chasm
that separates me from this:

what is called "France," what is called "Europe"

and also "Germany"

. . . and the boxes I have just emptied onto German soil are full, precisely, of these troubling oppressions, these shadows of time; they are terror itself, proof that the whole narrative I have devised for my new life, my flight, is false; spilling out the contents onto the ground is a way of opening up to memory and the past, and also of transgressing a family law, in a family that was always intent on hiding, hiding anything that trembled, but

the windows of time are not to be reopened

do you remember that, Jerome?

the eleventh commandment, which I must break; this law imprinted on the family after Talmaï's suicide; and I, the remaining brother, when I open the boxes, I don't know what I'm afraid of; I feel the oppressive weight of this law, but what is it we fear, coming to us from the past? are we frightened that order will waver, or that the matter crystallized around our silence will shatter on colliding with a particle of truth?

look at me, Jerome, I am afraid; I walk on a carpet of photographs from our childhood and I don't recognize us; I'm still bound by the law, the eleventh commandment, and I stop after the first gesture: spilling out the boxes, a sacrilege in which a person, sworn to the order of the secret—*not to reopen the windows of time*—tries to turn back; because he has no choice, because the pain is forcing him, his teeth are infected, his bones are cracked glass that will no longer bear his weight; there are so many pictures, my brother, most of them taken by the father back when life was easy and the "family" seemed able to provide for all our aspirations; to see you, my family, in this chaos of yellowing paper is to see the faces of those I spent the last years of the century with; without you, as I now understand, there would be no evidence of my life . . .

my King, help me if you're here, somewhere
in the heart of the Eastern winter

impart to me your acquiescing lips

tell me that I can break this law
transgress my family's order
my mother's and my father's

secrets that link the dead to each other, link fears

here an ancestor's suicide, there a brother's

give me strength, my King

to penetrate the silence and carry further
my research

let this genealogical quest
be a poem of renewed life

weeks pass; the city in the East wraps Theseus in its veil of shadows: the brother who is left fights pains that no doctor can explain; he is alone with the force that is crushing him; he makes himself go on walks, though his condition is against it: the teeth and dura mater are places where the shambles and impacts of a person's genealogy are encrypted; lower down, above his waist, a region the Chinese call the *dai mai*, the "belt meridian," the only horizontal channel linking heaven and earth, linking the mind's aerial flights and the body's base, a zone of junction and disjunction between those still to come, one's children, and those already gone, one's ancestors, in him is like the stem of a glass with a visible crack; it has stopped supporting him, and Theseus thinks

now everything is falling and life is accursed

but he fights on, held by the promise he exacted from his brother a few days before his death...

if you can't shake off your fears, Jerome, try to let the years take their course; time can accomplish what the will cannot; put yourself in time's hands; everything that you can't obtain by relying on your will, time can provide...

and the brother who died, Jerome, said to him that day: *I will not kill myself*, he'd given his word, but he didn't keep it; he'd been fighting for so many years, Jerome, against fears he didn't understand; just like the ancestor, Oved's father, when he'd written: *I won't shut myself away with him in a crypt*... Jerome hadn't kept his word, but Theseus that day had grabbed him by the hand:

you promise? you promise?

and so, to expel the rage and terror transmitted to him by the dead brother, he forces himself to walk his sick body outdoors; enters the parks of the city in the East to inhale the icy air; looks into the emaciated woods for hope and takes back with him some of the pale strength of trees so as to hold on; because walking reawakens his pains; and the days go by, but he isn't getting any better; returning home, he rereads the questions he has scribbled on a piece of paper over the pictures

who commits the murder of a man who kills himself?

and another that now
calls him

the one who survives, what story
is he intended to tell?

. . . he finds the photographs all around his bed, no longer takes the trouble to put them away; everything is falling, he thinks, but matter is patient: the trees know how to wait, and so do stones, lakes, rivers, photographs; we, though, are in such a hurry; we inflict on our bodies the sickly pulsation of our wants; he, for his part, wants to get well; as a *modern*, like his brother, Jerome, who was so impatient; he'd like for there to be a doctor, a drug, that would put him back on his feet; but life is *matter that knows*, matter that we'd like to decipher but about which, despite all our apparatus, we understand nothing; *matter imposes its rhythm, a wound takes its sweet time*, while we want rocks to speak and skin to heal; we are like trees that tremble in a storm; for now, falling, he tells himself to accept the time imposed by matter; the time required by the body falling, the photographs summoning the past; what else can he do but face up to the evidence, try to see if the images kick-start life in him, and in the meantime pretend to be?

because a man gives the impression of laughing
when everything draws him toward darkness

and that measures the degree of his internal flaw

the power to produce an appearance
when everything inside him

is dying

and maybe this power to appear, he thinks, this power to give *the impression of being alive*, is what allowed his brother, Jerome, to make that promise two days before he killed himself: *I won't kill myself*, because that's what you give others: a vow and a face that, somewhere deep inside, has already said goodbye; and if Theseus is holding on, it's also for that reason, so as not to betray, not add a wound to the wound . . .

they've confiscated death, he thinks,

I'm forced to hold on

so the brother who is left, Theseus, goes on walks attempting to pull himself together, to lift up the matter in him, because he wants to get well, *because you have to walk*, the doctors tell him, despite the pain, and the wound, and his frozen left side; and in the city's parks he inhales what the swaying trees have to offer: a bit of pale air and strength; then, once again home, he shuffles over the strewn photographs and lies down to stop the hurt; from his bed, where he spends all the remaining hours, he forces himself to connect with what wells up from the pictures: his childhood of joy and illusion; to look at the Ektachrome slides, a format that is no longer in use but

that his father loved, he has gotten hold of a viewer; and
the technology has an effect on him he hadn't expected

a light source that I can't find within me, he thinks,
is going to illuminate my life?

a bulb, nothing more than that, a bulb
to light the darkness and show me the way?

there were many days, as I've said, weeks even, of
stubborn opposition on all fronts; the matter in him
gave way, the bones, the tissue in his back collapsed;
and the useless doctors couldn't figure it out

it's in your head, they said, *we can't find anything*
in the X-rays, the ultrasounds, the MRIs

yet Theseus knows, he can swear to it, he's not making
up this illness; inside him it's tangible, a weight, souls
maybe, or the dead, or membranes that, to protect
him, because everything in him is a chemistry of fear,
have tightened up around his bones; in any case, the
belt around his *dai mai*, the meridian that the Chinese
associate with cracks in genealogy, seems on the point
of breaking; he is alone with his illegible body

he thinks

we are woven of language, and the body is the envelope
where everything mixes: the word and the tissues' chemistry . . .

we say "to carry one's family on one's back," and "to break down" or else "to hold"

and he asks himself *what is there to hang on to?*

where to find joy and lightness again
throw off this weight that is inside him
that is taking his strength

for now, he lies down among the pictures that he has brought in from the living room to his bed, the place where he lives all day; and he revisits scene after scene, the memories of his childhood, reweaves the thread that has been cut, hoping to emerge from the labyrinth; he hasn't seen the monster, can't *yet* see him; but he is investigating the deleted links, braving the prohibitions that his family was constrained by . . .

the windows of time are not to be reopened
don't ask questions about the forebear who wanted to die
leave everything in confusion, go toward the future

and his memory, he notices, is a bombed area that it is painful to revisit; he makes himself go there a little, forces himself, leaves everything lying on the floor so that it's in evidence when he returns; but reopening the archives of what has been—and the missing pictures of the hour when his brother hanged himself, when his mother fell asleep never to wake again, when his father left him, talking about a black page with no visible top or bottom—he falls even further . . .

he writes

I search the past for evidence of my own life

and also to get well

but who kills a person who has decided to die?

and the one who survives, what story is he intended to tell?

these questions won't let him go; he'd like to twist them into a torch to light his way across this uncharted crypt, along the path he must take as night sets in;
he raises himself from his bed to search through the pictures, wonders where he should start; at this point, he has not yet read the manuscript by Talmaï, his ancestor, and nothing makes sense; he hasn't yet given himself permission to probe the past; and medicine, the science of *the moderns*, is flummoxed; he looks

at a picture, looks at another; searches for a clue to start from; he stares at photographs of his father, his mother; but none of it means anything; and suddenly, it strikes him: *I should start here*, he thinks, here with this picture he is holding, where a young man and a young woman are getting married

there, he thinks, everything was still possible
including what seems so crazy when looked at from the future
that I might not be born, my brother either

that we might have stayed in limbo

if, on that day, he could have whispered a few words to his parents

don't do it, don't get married, or if you get married
leave us out of this life
forget procreation . . .

the first cracks

1969–2005

yet it had all started off so well; the father and
the mother were so talented, so good-looking, so
resplendent, their wedding was a dream, the dream
of a whole era; on them was projected, but as scenery,
the expectation of a world to come; there are so many
photographs, so many films of their wedding; they
represented a promise, and Nathaniel, the father of
the bride, son of the ancestor, who considered himself
a leftist and who attacked the bourgeoisie's interests
by supporting the youth movement in 1968, led them
onto a boat that had been bought for the occasion;
imagine that, a boat for their wedding; and a sweeping
bridal train, a cherubic children's choir, the garden
smartly clipped, the lake a mirror reflecting the bride...
a dream, as I say; and in the background, the Thirty
Glorious Years of prosperity, the war receding in
memory, 1969, a year of love... and you, the young
fiancé, the future husband, my father, your diplomas
destined you to a prodigious life; you, my mother, the
modern girl, were promised great success...

didn't I neglect my children
for my work life?

it would be one of the questions that haunted you after your son's suicide; I never felt that the father, your young fiancé, asked himself those questions; but what did you do, the mother, that your life collapsed as it did, what did you bungle, dear parents, by looking only toward the future? do you see it all more clearly now that you are dead? in the photographs, on that day flush with sunlight, the bride is a swan, the water is calm . . . everything seems to be blessing you: the flowers, the mountains . . . the boat's wake is a blade slicing the silk of the water; the bride smiles; swiveling her hands, she greets the accompanying crowd; the families are there, the friends, the people of Nathaniel, the son of the forebear; it would seem that he's managed to turn the page, as society has apparently done too; *because you have to forget and make no mention of Talmaï, the bullet to the brain and the unkept promise after the death of the child who wanted to be king, it's best to forget, to remain forgetful, of where you come from, of the prayers you haven't learned, you have to be French, a French success story*, and Nathaniel will not speak about the past; he marries off his daughter, and the rest is ancient history; here, in this society, in 1969, so far from the procession of shadows, so far from Vichy, so far from the cravenness of the French, the alliance that fell through, the assimilated citizens stripped of their nationality, so far from the heinousness of Germany, from the Wannsee lake, where Theseus's children would go swimming in the city in the East, so far from the two wars where people slaughtered each other, where Europe conducted exterminations, where power slashed indiscriminately between clean and dirty, life and death, humanity and the old prayer that Oved wanted to say; in 1969, with their eyes turned toward America, toward the *beat* from the United States, they followed an ascending path; they kept quiet about people's origins, about the tangle of beliefs, languages, memories, and suspicions that German history and the French police hacked at to divide name from name; Nathaniel would say nothing about his father, who committed suicide, nothing about Oved and the Jewish prayer; that would have to wait for "Jerome," which is the brother's name, "Jerome" . . .

because for now

the myth being transmitted is of separate lives

of the ancestor's sorrow, which carried him off,

of a French life,

of the past that is buried, the present that is taking wing

of eras imagined
as milestones

along a road leading forward

war, war

ruins and collapse, then

rebuilding

twenty-five years after the cessation of hostilities and the German surrender, Nathaniel, the father of the bride, the son of the ancestor, the brother of young Oved, thinks only of the future, of which you are the bodies; for you and your generation, he will be the "leftist boss," if such a thing can be; but it can't, of course, and it's not because he's a "boss"; it's humanity as a whole that is tragically mad, the whole life we're leading that's an aberration; the least little bit of power is now too much; I know it, living as I do in this aftertime and having seen you fall; but Nathaniel, you have to understand, is the son of the dead man, orphaned of his father, the child of a fragility that is left unspoken; and in the place of emptiness, of terror, he brings life, movement, willpower; his successes are the answer that resilience gives to death, that the son makes so his father will take notice even from the afterlife; and in those days that was the energy, the energy of resilience . . .

1950 . . . 1960 . . .
everything had to be rebuilt on new foundations
on the myth of well-being, of French prosperity,
prosperity across Europe

you had to go fast, you had to want, consume, produce; there, by the lake, your wedding was a fairy tale of modernity; the war orphans' triumph, the spirit of the Great Rebuild, and Nathaniel, who was stage-managing, greeted the guests and erased the old wounds with a wave of his industrial wand . . .

there are no Jews, no Christians
we celebrate the melting pot of a reconciled France
its hatreds left behind

the year is 1969, and look, all eyes are turned toward America, and you, there by the lake, you're the birth of the cool bourgeoisie; that same sense of *cool* that we see in *cool jazz* and *cool bebop*; a France that, rather than look at its murky or tainted aspects, turns toward the West and U.S. pop culture; the music takes after *Hair*, the musical; the way people look borrows from the Kennedys: there's a rhythm and a style that I find everywhere in the pictures, corresponding to your *Trente Glorieuses*, your thirty golden years, that age of abundance in whose ruins we grew up; and you, the children of that furious age whose growth devoured the world, look how you were loved: you're a model couple, you point to success in a France that, by all accounts, has broken with the cycle of its shame...

that is the French fiction you play out
my dear little parents

1969... you are returning from life on a college campus in California; that country changed you; the injustice of the Vietnam War... the rules of baseball... the laws of *new* management... *new* journalism... all that novelty... your eyes look into space... tears shed on a grassy knoll in Dallas... the Reverend Martin Luther King... a few ideas for the music that will be played tonight... 1969, suits are still pressed, bangs are combed; but my question is, how will your vibration as moderns help me get through the archaism of death? what good are your pervasive 1960s and 1970s in the ruins you left me? and what does your heroic tale of French success have to offer the one who remains?

you don't answer, my dear little parents, for in the prosperous life of your youth, the dead have no voice; the two of you go no further than being an announcement; the guests applaud you, you say your "yes" to each other, a *yes* that I'll come back to because I know what came of it: us, born of your aspirations, your myths . . .

"the desires of your era are a tomb"

that is what occurs to me as I look at you

amid the ruin, the collapse

from which I see you

and already, yes, the era of infinite energy is past; the crisis will be for us, your children; we won't have a right to forward progress: oil, prosperity, growth . . . our cycle will be one of leftovers, of making do with what falls from the enchanted and illusory parenthesis of your youth; our time will be one in which wounds reopen; but in the archived record of the wedding, no one is suffering, no, there is laughter; Nathaniel, the ancestor's son, was so important to the mother; she needed him to be strong, to approve of the husband, my father; and he did organize this wedding all for her; he made it a choreography of forgetting, a cover-up moment, an abduction from the memory palace, an image constructed to erase History, obliterate pain, celebrate life, and above all stop thinking of death; who on that day would have dared mention Talmaï? thirty years had gone by—1939–69—and a new epoch had arrived; from this point on, we were making it up; religion, prayer, and faith belonged to the past, we were manufacturing joy; and as I immerse myself in your wedding album, my father's words come back to me

he said

those were high times!

words he punctuated with others that made him
laugh hard

we lived in the grand style!

quite right, dear parents,
you carried on up in the stratosphere, but I wonder
if you ever considered
the coming down . . .

because, look, fifty years after your wedding, I am lying in a bedroom in the city in the East, where I've chosen to live to escape you; the bones in my back no longer support me, my lymph channels are blocked, and my nervous system has gone haywire; there is in me a kind of body that I can feel, and it's crushing me; your sick pictures are spread out around my bed; the winter is full of rain, and I'm examining this evidence of past life; one image among many speaks to me; you the father and you the mother are sitting on a rocky prominence, seemingly in the high mountains; I pick up the picture to find an inscription on the back in your hand, the mother, saying that three years have elapsed since your wedding

and I write

the black waters of time need to be cleansed and the dead healed, if such a thing can be; there has to be a return to the time that engendered all of this, a look at the flip side of your promises, a hole poked in the stage sets where you raised us; stage sets death has pierced, leaving me surrounded by your ruins . . .

. . . and here is what you, the mother, wrote in captioning the picture: summer 1972; if the chronology can be trusted, the birth date of your first son is approaching—January 26, 1973; that summer is a suspended time before you fatally became father and mother, because I know, now

we are not isolated bodies

nor separate minds

matter carries a memory, an intelligence, that is vaster
that connects us

we are a continuous flux of appearances and disappearances
crossed with a thousand disasters

but in those days when I discovered your picture, I knew nothing, understood nothing; I was only aware that what was being intimated on that rock, the possible, the hoped for, *your first child*, was now dead; that summer of 1972, my dear little parents, saw the first months of a pregnancy that would lead to January 26, 1973; and, like a mirror, because life apparently is an arithmetic operation that no one can unravel, that same date of January 26 but thirty-three years later would be the day on which your body, the mother, would give out; because I, who visit you from the future, know that you are no more; and what specialist of vibration physics will look into these dates, when everything seems called to mirror itself?

my dear parents, what's troubling you
on this rock, in the summer of 1972?

do you have a foreboding about the mechanism grinding
to a start
with the child on its way?

has it come, the great fear that would overtake you
that you would bury under the glorious fiction
of your French life

your Parisian successes?

you are bringing a child into the world in THIS world,
taking that risk!

creating "Jerome," burdening him with your silences
with all you think you've escaped:

History, what cuts in History
starting from what's killed

each of your scripts, so full of the fear of losing
losing a father, losing a son

fears that "Jerome," the translator,
would have to suture together

for me, looking at you, the possibilities have shut down; I know what the brother looks like on the red floor tiles when his stiff, cold body has been cut down; I know that he was born, that he killed himself in his thirty-third year; and you, the mother, what do you say about the date on which your body gave out, the anniversary of your son's birth? should it be seen as an admission, an eagerness to join him, or proof that you never managed to separate yourself from him? I've read that adepts of psychogenealogy call that *synchrony*, when the calendar contrives to hit the living over the head; a son is born, a mother dies, and between those dates when the son comes into being and the mother falls asleep on a bus never to wake up, all the secrets of our body-memories . . .

what is it in the repetition of these dates?

what fragility lies behind the glorious fiction?

why does the brother kill himself on March 1?

what sense is to be made of all these numbers?
how does one not go crazy?

how is one to live again, after all your camouflaging,
your spending?

how will I manage to clean these murky waters
you left me in?

here's what the brother who is left has to do: understand why Jerome hanged himself, get himself back together after his fall, shine a light on what you were blind to, listen to his body, which knows more than we do, work out how lives intersect and why no one can say: *I'll pull through all on my own*; and so as to cast light on this rope linking one era to another I ask myself . . .

is this why I fell,
why the body dragged me down?

is there a reason for the wound?

was it to make me face up to the pictures and conduct my investigation?

is the wound God?

that is

the locus of necessity in human substance?

you, my dear parents, who were busy making a splash in Paris, put us in the hands of a substitute mother, a woman paid to care for us seven days a week, twenty-four hours a day, and look: you succeeded in your careers, you took all the light, all the energy, and what did you leave in your wake? futile discussions of socialism, of the latest reshuffling of the French establishment, whose spear tip you were . . . X is coming to dinner, Y will join us tomorrow night . . . the good life of an elite in its ascendancy, of its children, who study foreign languages so the order will persist . . .

is that why I fell?

so as not to replicate your Parisian careers?

so as to fail?

is that why I left?

to flee the West and its murderous modern ways

and to search in the East

for other forms of knowledge, more archaic, revisiting there,
in the silence
the history of the wound?

. . . look, my dear little parents, I'm in the city in the East and I'm falling; I'm trying to penetrate the mystery of your glory days; I've given myself over to the monster, to the darkness in us that tries to work itself into the world; I'm trying to decipher what there is to decipher and I've surrendered to night; I would like to not repeat, to break the future's spell; and so I've reopened the boxes that I considered destroying: I consent to confronting the past to see the diagonal incised into the bark of time; and if I can trust that date—summer 1972, when the two of you were sitting there like children on your rock—then the mother must have been pregnant with the son who was to come: Do you talk under the white sky about the unborn child? you both look so serious: you, the mother, are pinching your nails; I recognize it as the gesture with which you'd pick at your clear, pearlescent nail polish, *because red nail polish is for girls*, you used to say; and I can see that in this picture you avoid each other's eyes; I can guess what underlies this silence, but should I fill it in with what I've learned?

should this child be born?

six months before your due date, the mother, that's the question on your mind: *Should this child be born?* I write it to understand what there might be inside Jerome, my brother, that would tremble; he would be the first boy in the maternal line, Nathaniel's eldest grandson, Jerome, a third-generation descendant of the ancestor; and his chance of existing hangs on a thread; because you told me, mother, that the doctors predicted complications; there was an illness that might make the son *a fragile man*; and in this family, *fragile men . . .*

they kill themselves, mother

they die turning toward heaven

searching for the words of a forgotten prayer

"Baruch atah Adonai . . ."

the one I had to relearn so as not, on the day of my death,
to find myself mute

like Oved, the boy who wanted to be
the first Jewish king of France

but you know nothing, the mother, no one has told you anything; you're unaware of the past; your life grew out of the great cover-up of the postwar years, when France ran away from the things it had done, from those it had summarily sent to the camps in the East, that same France that didn't surrender, didn't knuckle under, no, because it forestalled infamy and German demands by offering up its children to death; you know nothing of this *Jewish history*, nothing of the prayer, nothing of what is left unspoken in the family of your young husband; no, because you're a baby boomer, looking in 1969 toward the future; and now you're fighting for your son to be born: you stand up to the male voices—your father Nathaniel's first among them, who agrees with the doctors' advice and wants you to abort; we're still in that time when women's bodies were treated as the property of men and girls were submitted to their father's authority; but sitting on this rock, you have a decision to make . . .

should "JEROME" be born?

should the postwar story be sutured together?

the myth of rebuilding France and the shadows of the past,

the dead of your lineage?

. . . I turn to the lindens in front of my window, and I think about what you're feeling, you, the mother; your solitude, and that pocket of worry in you where the brother is taking shape; the chorus of doctors who say: *you must abort*, then there's your young husband, who doesn't know what to think, who has somber ideas; he talks about capitalism, which is destroying the Earth, about nuclear war, which almost erupted in the early 1960s; he already senses what's to come, the permanent state of emergency after the decades of abundance: the depletion of resources, the destruction of species, the melting of the permafrost . . . he lacks only the ability to see what is wavering inside him; he camouflages it all by identifying his qualms with great catastrophes

so this is what was happening at the end of your

thirty glorious postwar years:

you, daughter of a secret, carrying unawares

the loss of a child who wanted to be king

Oved

the FIRST JEWISH KING OF FRANCE

and your husband, "Gatsby," as he was known,
orphaned of his father

something is there, at the beginning, that gets into "Jerome,"

an unnoticed fragility, unspoken fears,

whose burden I carry

but Gatsby doesn't want to know, he hides, he dissembles, that's how men are; he was born at the end of the war, November 30, 1944, and he doesn't know that the ancestor, in the maternal line, killed himself on November 30 in the year 1939; another *synchronicity*, but no one picks up on it; who reads your story for what the days have to say? the father, Gatsby, makes speeches on how growth needs to be checked; catastrophe is a landscape where he puts all the things concealed in him; his anxieties as an orphan, which he camouflages, he turns into politics; and I'm telling you this why, you, the mother? because it will all come out when your son Jerome starts to tremble; and after him . . . it will be my turn; once you're gone, I'll be pulled groundward by forces I'm trying to stare down; but I need to check off the clues one by one to reconstruct a crime scene: the letters, the photographs, what's left of you . . .

you'll be surprised, my dear little parents,
at what I've discovered

and it may be why I'm in pieces
forced to live lying down

seeing the cracks in human matter

becoming the eyes that observe you from the future

being the domino that stays standing in a family that falls

obstinately questioning:

who commits the murder of a man who kills himself?

and the one who survives, what story
is he intended to tell?

. . . if you'd had more time, the mother, would you have understood what connects lives, one to another? the flow in our memories that joins eras together and the trickling of the past into the present, so that what plays out in our mysteries is the future itself; if you had lived, but you died so young, at fifty-nine; and in the last years you started to write articles about war; you tried to interview Nuremberg judges, camp survivors, soldiers from the Great War; little by little, you were opening the doors to the past; you were breaking the eleventh commandment

the windows of time are not to be reopened

you didn't know it, but you were starting off down this path, the one I'm following, where interpenetrating ghosts are haunting, secrets glisten moistly; people often live on a single plane of existence, the one where they read the papers, sleep, work, go on vacation; but there is also a second plane, the one where something is working itself out in a flux that washes through people's bodies; and you, mother, were searching, but as a blind man does; instead of looking at the heart of man's fear; instead of retracing the path where Oved's unfound prayers, and Talmaï's terrors, and Nathaniel's glory join together, you were looking elsewhere; you were writing articles about the infantrymen of the Great War, about the Resistance fighters; I kept those articles, they're here on the floor, with all the rest; and I can see that your journalist's gaze was zeroing in at the end; because everything in you must have known that you had to search in that direction, those dark hours when the sounds of a war already just about lost drowned out the pistol shot that Talmaï directed at himself, making *a small red hole in his right temple* but there was the law, your family's commandment

the windows of time are not to be reopened

that was imprinted in the bodies of the descendants immediately following Talmaï's death; and so, instead of the gentle speech in Oved's memory, instead of the words of the errant text suggesting dance and a return to life, instead of prayers that might have reconnected us to God, we would be treated to silence and the acting out of success; for the law is the law, and it says that you, the mother, shouldn't look back; you wanted to write about the shades of French collaboration, *that other procession*; you sensed that that's where you needed to go, toward the silences, but your son was losing his footing; he was going deeper into the night, and you'd have liked to help him; with all your mother's heart, you'd have liked to help him; but you obeyed the law, you were not allowed to investigate, no, that was forbidden, you would not read us the story of Oved, the boy who wanted to be king...

by rights, you should have confronted the fear that comes over men

but I see it now

rather than display their trembling

men prefer to fight or commit suicide

and I will have to cross through death, learn to say

"I am trembling, I'm afraid and I don't want to die"

my dear parents, when I've cleared away the shapeless mass of this archive, I'll tell you about it; for the moment, I know nothing, I understand nothing; and to you, the mother, I can say only that you weren't a help to me; you left out so much, rearranged things so much to maintain the legend of your wonderful family, your beautiful children; but understand, I'm not reproaching you; I know that the law was in force and only the myth could be told . . .

but tell me, when did you start to see the cracks
in the father?

sense the fear that would overtake you

when Gatsby started to waver?

know all that would befall once that resilient man,

the pillar of your life, Nathaniel, the ancestor's son,

turned away from him?

. . . you the mother, see how I am still sorting through things and not figuring it out; for the moment I see nothing but indictments going against the grain of time, complaints not from me but from you; I sense that there is something linking different eras to each other; I sense that with Oved a knot started to form, from the ancestor's keen sorrow, his suicide, and from the subsequent injunction to silence; I have dates, synchronicities: January 26, the date of your death thirty-three years to the day after the birth of your son; November 30, the ancestor's suicide, that resonates with the birth of the man who would become my father, the so-called Gatsby; watch, the mother, while I dive deep into the jumbled archives that I brought with me, read the errant Kaddish that Talmaï dedicated to his history-loving child; I live in the midst of all these images scattered on the floor; I try to make sense of it, but there is resistance, darkness, in my inflamed bones, my back, which breaks down when I most want to forget it; you didn't help me, the mother, but I don't hold it against you; I just want to cut the bonds that pull me to the ground and live again . . .

. . . still sprawled on my bed in the city in the East, searching through the photos on the floor, I'm struck by another picture from your wedding; so I'm back in the summer of 1969, the day of your union, the day everything became irreversible; because it was then you started to form the stubborn notion of *giving*

birth; you clung to the notion, against the advice of Nathaniel and the doctors, overriding the fears of your young husband, who had been attentively following the warnings about our industrial production models issued by the Club of Rome; your husband who, three years later, and a few months before the birth of your first son, Jerome, would read the "Meadows Report" . . .

The Limits to Growth

1972

a report commissioned by MIT,
the research lab at
the Massachusetts Institute of Technology,

presenting computer simulations of the consequences
of economic growth and our human systems,
technology, and economic activity for the Earth System

and in this photograph, in the blank space between you, I seem to see Nathaniel, the ancestor's son; if we belonged to an Italian family—I'm thinking of those *men of honor* that the movies linger over to show what clans are made of—the honor code, the inevitable trials for treachery—I'd call him the boss of your *cosa*, the one who holds the *famiglia* together; and in fact Italy is not altogether absent from the photos of your wedding:

the boutonnieres of roses, the three-piece suits . . . your wedding dress, mother, disappears into the white of daylight, and Nathaniel, your father, at a distance, bends down: the gesture is clear: you, the young husband, my father, in this other photograph, hold out your glass at this moment when you are entering the clan; your eyes look at the glass into which champagne is being poured from outside the frame . . .

the "Meadows Report" stressed the need
to put a stop to growth:

on the demographic front, the report's authors
argue for a limit of two children per couple

and on the economic front, they recommend
taxing industry to combat
pollution

and I suspect that this toast, this instant when you are clinking glasses, happens afterward; I can't imagine you doing it *before*; if the bride and groom had drunk *before*, your union might have been declared null and void; it could be challenged on the grounds that the *yes* of the bride and groom were spoken in a haze of inebriation; but everything, as I've said, had to be irreversible: your union, and all the years that intervened between that date, 1969, and the point in the future from which I look at you; and even if I wanted to annul your marriage and our birth, the brother's and mine, and your lies, the mother, and your various arrangements—*such a lovely couple, such a lovely family*—and the move to Paris, which removed me from a life surrounded by forests, far from the sophistications of the city; even if I wanted to erase this life that owed so much to power; and my brother's fears and the indictment he leveled at you later, and the *famiglia*'s violence, the words spoken about the dead behind their backs, to construct a story that would let nothing change; even if I wanted to stop what is foreshadowed here and the growth and destruction it caused, or the success myths that France perpetuates to shore up its pretenses, I couldn't; because time is time, and you didn't drink *before* but *after*; and you believe your *yes* to have been freely and advisedly given; but when I see this image, I think...

what if this wedding, rather than a wedding,

were a business contract

an extension of production by other means

a masterpiece of industrial control

over affective life and reproduction

to create two prototypes:

Jerome and Theseus, your children, us

two lives born of France's
fictions

. . . he, Nathaniel, to whom joy and fortune were given, stands between you; he was born in 1917, the year of the Russian Revolution; but he is not thinking now about Communism, or Oved, or his father the ancestor; he is 52 in 1969, in the prime of his life; he greets, he plays the host, he is forging what will become an empire; he has turned the silences into joy, the sorrows of the past into adventure; Nathaniel is strong, joyous, attentive; tomorrow, *he will feed all of France*; he hadn't joined the revolution exactly, but he was shrewd, that's for sure; he sensed what was in the offing: a more even distribution of the fruits of growth, and a different way of looking at work; he was attentive to the rumble of discontent, the call for change; during the months before the wedding, he went into the streets to hear the students' slogans; he visited the workers in his factories; and this was at a time when de Gaulle had just resigned; it was the first summer of an era that would leave the traumas of the past behind, the wars of decolonization, the old tensions; those who believed the world had been a better place before found themselves silenced; the *sense of the future* was against them; in their place came those who believed in transformation; Nathaniel was one of them; at least, he embodied a certain projection of the future: more freedom, an unmuzzled media, higher wages, a shorter workweek; and in this photograph, he is pouring champagne between Gatsby, my father, and you, the mother; if I were directing actors in a scene, I would say . . .

smile, you've just signed
your "reproductive contract"

you, the bridegroom, known as "Gatsby," are a brilliant young man who has just graduated from one of the grandes écoles, *one of the top-flight graduate programs in France; you then went to Stanford University, in the U.S., to put the finishing touches on your education; you speak English like an American; and together, my little parents, you think of yourselves as a promise, you're joining forces, you think that's what holds you together, love and forward momentum; you were born into the upper bourgeoisie, a fact that you don't hide, but you are not conservatives; you idealize what you saw in*

America; you think that during your short exile you were granted a concept of the future; you were marked by the magic bullet and the atomic bomb; but right now you try not to think of it too much; your families like each other, both want to see you married; you accept their blessing and give little thought to what went on before; the two of you marry, needless to say, as CHRISTIANS, so that the secret can live on, so that the Marranist story won't end, so that the cracks won't show, cracks that connect you; but you, blinder still, marry as "moderns"...

I'm not in a position to direct anyone, of course, and the film has already been released; with both of you having died, I'm at best a documentarian gathering material from the archives to establish what, at the time the film was shot, was ill-conceived; in your French fiction, my dear parents, I'm looking for the continuity lapses, the jump cuts, the missing dialogue; just where and when the perfect screenplay of your French life went off the rails; I'm proofreading, if you will, an overly produced and slightly doctored film; and, staring at the pictures on the carpet in the city in the East, I have to convince myself that the film is *real*, that certain people died in it; I have to accept the vitality of your union and the sandcastle of your French life; don't we say a *marriage contract*? and when you close a business deal, isn't it customary to raise a toast? here you are sealing the deal from which we were generated, my brother and I; I say this without in any way denying the love that I know to have bound you, but there's this fatality that I'm trying to grasp: you, the father, let's remember, were born on November 30; and you, the mother, were beguiled by a man whose birthday echoes the secret of the ancestor's suicide on November 30; and between those two dates, between 1939 and 1944, here's what happened: the erasure, the obliteration of the family's Jewish name . . .

what is modern *in all of this?*

and the happy story of Success, of Progress

of Nathaniel's industrial genius

the bet he placed on the young
"Gatsby"

what was developing that day between the two of you

what am I to think of it

living as I do in the wreckage of the world you built

you left?

and Joan Baez, Bob Dylan, the Beatles, JFK, and Martin Luther King, and the peace activists, and the dreams of the future that came out of that blessed time, did they manage to change the archaic flood that passes through bodies? the baby boomers held the floor for decades; they repeated the same refrain over and over about living large, they imposed their mimetic American values on everyone; they celebrated their age unrelentingly, to the point of confiscating the idea of youth for themselves right to the point of death; I'm not saying this about you specifically, my dear parents, I'm establishing the context of the 1960s, the 1970s . . . when everything was so overappreciated it became a turning point in history: the time when appetitive urban life and the revolution invented the era that followed; but from the perspective of the future, from a time when species are disappearing, megalopolises are swallowing up the Earth, and your cool capitalism of subcultures has lost all its ideals except ensuring its own preservation, what good is the narcissism of your era? and this change, this turn that you brought about, what does it have to offer us? and what can I expect from your *modernity* when everything I need to know has to do with just surviving?

I'm looking back at the summer of 1969, when it all started, my dear parents, and I'm trying to understand what's sweeping you along: the young bride and you, her dashing *husband*, you both believe in the movie about your love; on this day when you are being feted, no one is talking about shadows, secrets; no one is mentioning that at sixteen, you Gatsby, the young fiancé, lost your father; no one is talking about what it is that connects men, stemming from fear, loss, war, and destruction . . . for me, from the perspective of the future, your marriage looks like a broken promise; I look at you in the picture I'm holding in my hand, you're standing on the float a few minutes after saying your *yes*; in the corner is the young woman, in the center Nathaniel, on the left the son-in-law, young "Gatsby," and in the heart of your trio, the fragilities carefully hidden; because the era is one that embraces forgetting, and there had been the period when the two of you met, then the period of study in America, where the young man took shape . . .

this guy, Gatsby, is a hit!

in San Francisco's streets, do you remember, father, what you used to tell me?

"They would ask me to sign autographs, people took me for Dustin Hoffman."

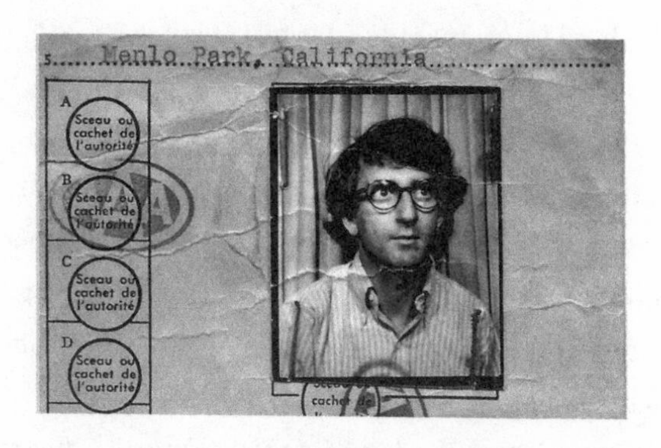

... the young woman follows you, not wanting to lose you; there in America, on the West Coast, your French life is a long way off, and the pact is made: you become engaged while in California, and everything follows from there; on your return, Gatsby, the youngest of a fatherless family, marries Esther, the daughter of Nathaniel the resilient, the luminous; and why this union? I would understand later, my dear little parents; I would peer, out of necessity, into the corners of your cracked fairy tale; I would search for the fragility lingering under the story of strength; but for the moment, I see nothing; I reopen my archives, lose my way; I find you happy in the pictures, a happiness that strikes me as a fiction from start to finish; and yet I know that for ten years, the trio you formed held together; Nathaniel, the father of the bride, laughed with Gatsby, and the daughter, Esther, took delight in their friendship; I have no memory of these carefree years, but I know that the energy waned: you told me about it, father: the price of oil shot up, and the crisis startled a world that had grown complacent; the factories that Nathaniel ran had to be sold—glass factories and bottling plants—and you were assigned to sell off this past, Gatsby; at that point something changed in the way the resilient one, Nathaniel, looked at you; he saw you as fragile, affected by having to carry out this task, and in his family, fragility meant problems . . .

a man who trembles is a reminder of that day of violence
when the ancestor was found

Talmaï

with a little hole in his right temple

November 30, 1939,

a memory that comes under the law

"the windows of time are not to be reopened"

Nathaniel says to his friends and family:
"it's all about willpower and work"

but the young woman, Esther, doesn't know why
this husband who is weakening worries her

she draws away from him, as animals do

she asks herself: is it possible he won't hold out?
will he measure up to my father?

alone, I, Theseus, your last son, lying collapsed in the city in the East, understand not a thing; I've only managed to open some boxes of pictures, but I ask myself: who in this family has dared show anything but strength? and the fragility of my father, my brother, where did it come from? and these fears that flatten me? I don't know what to say, so to get away from your dead lives, I turn toward the window; as I watch, the last leaf of a skeletal linden tree falls to the ground; for a moment I have the sensation of fluttering down in its place; for a few seconds, I am the soul of the last leaf on the linden in front of my window, and believe it or not, my dear little parents, I begin to cry; because the son who is left no longer sees any way out, he is concerned that he won't be able to get up, he fears that he will offer his children only the sight of a body carried off by darkness . . .

> *I'm not finding my way out of this, and I'm not getting any better; I go see doctors who don't understand a thing; I go see shamans who read strange omens in the sky; am I going to get back on my feet? they say that something in me has to die; that it falls to certain people to cleanse time; I listen to them, but I don't understand, and I stay with your pictures or the ancestor's manuscript; when I'd finally read this text in Oved's memory, the promises of this great-grandfather who, like Zweig, decided to kill himself at midcentury, I told myself I should take this piece of writing, which tries to soften our grief, as my starting point; but the pains don't fall away, and nothing in me is repaired; the photos at my feet are knife blades, and the shamans that I visit out of despair—because the doctors offer no remedy—tell me that the pain in my temples is the bullet that entered the skull of Talmaï, the father of the child who wanted to be king*

. . . and despite this body-memory, because I have children that I am watching grow up, I persist; I go back to the images, I plunge my hands among them as into the waters of time; I try to reconstruct a framework, to summarize life; to penetrate the wall that I've erected between me and the past; I come back to the years following your wedding; I know that the times twist out of shape, that everything gets harder, more painful; the 1973 oil crisis comes along, and everything seems to go awry; and you two, the father and the mother, under Nathaniel's eye, start a family; you have one child, then another; I, the brother who is left, am the second; and your life, from the outside, seems fairly successful; there's a house that your sons grow up in; you are moderns, progressives, close to the young Turks of the socialist party who, along with François Mitterrand, are coming into power; you have good diplomas, you've come back from America, and you work hard, while others are off taking drugs . . .

I'm going to be a journalist

you'd said that, Esther, since childhood, I have proof of it on the floor; the newspapers you created are lying there, little notebooks of sixteen pages that you so precociously divided into sections and that speak to your determination; you, the mother, knew that you would be a journalist from your tenderest age; and now you have children, two boys, but you don't let anything go, give anything up; you're hired by *France-Soir*, where you work the night shift; business reporting is your chosen field, or maybe your fate; you should be putting questions to Nathaniel, "the Leftist boss," probing the secret he was raised within, the fears he never mentions; but instead of that, no, you do your classwork; you interview other bosses, hundreds of them, but never your father; you go off on assignments, start to develop a certain idea of the French *success story*; you're young, but you keep your promise: *I won't be a homebody, I'll earn my freedom*; in that respect, you belong very much to your time, have the courage to defy the old males . . .

I had to fight, you'd tell me,
to survive in my profession, as a woman,
I really had to fight . . .

and as for the father, Gatsby,

he lost his own father at the age of sixteen, and repressing his grief so thoroughly he was unaware of it, looked for protection; he formed a friendship with a boy from a family less grief-stricken than his own, and this friend turned out to have a slender and attractive sister whom he came to know; Esther, for that was her name, grew to like him; that's how he entered the life of the woman who would become his wife; and Nathaniel, the father, offered him work . . .

. . . after graduating, Gatsby made several attempts to go his own way, then accepted Nathaniel's offer of a position; he went to work for the company and unwittingly joined the lineage of men who die; in those pioneering years, he worked for an empire under construction; the business still consisted of glassworks, heavy industry, factories smelling of oil and fire; and as Gatsby had a solid set of diplomas and a grounding in American *management*, he was able to assume a position as a senior strategist; he rose quickly, generated reports, participated as an adviser in the decisions of the boss, the resilient, luminous Nathaniel; there was one episode that he would remember to his last breath; 1972, the oil crisis still lay ahead, son Jerome had not yet been born; the world that had emerged victorious from the hell of war and atomic destruction still believed in unending growth; and young Gatsby, who was part of the select group of *advisers*, contributed to the writing of the *Marseille speech . . .*

there is only one Earth

said Nathaniel, using words composed for him by Gatsby

the date is October 25, 1972,

economic growth and the market economy have utterly transformed
living standards in the Western world
this is undeniable

but the result is far from perfect

first because this growth does not guarantee justice

too many people still live below
an acceptable standard of well-being, both in the nation and the business environment

we cannot allow growth
to leave so many outcasts behind:
the elderly, the handicapped, the ill, and especially those many
workers who share inadequately
in the fruits of prosperity

and this growth engenders noxious effects
both collective and individual

it sacrifices environmental concerns and working conditions
to economic efficiency

and that is why it is controversial and sometimes rejected as the end goal
of the industrial era

should we allow this to go on? continue having confidence in the market?

it would lead us inevitably to revolution

we must set ourselves human and social goals

is this not a challenge we can accept?

there were many setbacks in my father's life, but the *Marseille speech* was his great pride: from the shadows, Gatsby had contributed modestly to the development of what he would call, right up to his death, *capitalism with a human face*; those are your words, father, do you remember? and to think that so many—members of labor unions, political parties, businesses—joined in with this belief but as you know, Gatsby, and as you would say again and again in the last years of your life: the catastrophe has our name on it; at the top are those whom the power structure favors; those who devour the Earth, who accumulate and confiscate; there is no *capitalism with a human face*; capitalism, now, is the other name for *Homo sapiens*, the name for the fictions we use to govern the world, the name of ruin; and as visionary as this speech was that you helped write, think through, and have delivered in Nathaniel's voice, it didn't stop anything; not the expansion of capital, not the profligate use of global resources; we humans, father, pay ourselves with words: language and the stories it weaves produce captivating narratives; you believed in the *speech*, the words spoken by Nathaniel the resilient, Esther's father, the hero of the Thirty Glorious Postwar Years, who started in the glassmaking industry and ended up feeding the world, by *sugarcoating* it; Nathaniel, the one who for a time embodied *French modernity*; but isn't that what we know best how to do: believe? we like to be lulled by belief, the total sorcery of language; a *speech*, what can a *speech* do? what value would the words "justice," "Earth," and "outcasts" have a few months later, in October 1973, when the oil-producing countries that had till then been pawning

their deserts to supply the energy needs of a few
northern Whites jacked up the bill?

the speeches were left behind, my dear little dad,
and the crisis took hold; something eroded between
you, your young wife, and Nathaniel; he put you
in charge, as I said, of selling off the old factories,
because the winds were shifting; 1973, 1974, 1975,
and then 1976, the year of the great drought, which
was also the year of my birth; and there was no longer
unlimited energy; time to forget the promises made
in the *speech*; although you agreed with the Club of
Rome's recommendations, dreamed of transforming
the old capitalism, promoting the ideal of zero growth,
you no longer had the time to redesign our way of
life; Nathaniel assigned you a role, not as a strategist
this time but as an operative; he wanted to test
you in action, see how you performed in difficult
circumstances; you had to find buyers who were naive
enough to believe in the old heavy industry; your

job was to sell them factories poised for decline and abandonment; you'd wanted the future, you'd gone to America to get away from *archaism*; but here you were responsible for selling off old accounts, a few dying branches that Nathaniel was jettisoning so that his empire would survive; you were shutting down, selling; and this strategy—getting rid of what's dying—was a task you found it difficult to perform; at the start of the 1980s, we'd been through two oil crises, I was four years old and Jerome, my brother, was seven, and you quit the business; the scene featuring your little trio was starting to break apart . . .

so that's what I have then, the start of a story, the story of your falling out of love, of this 1969 union that fell apart over the years; the head of the family saw you as a successor, almost a son, and yet you left him; the glorious trio that you formed in that sunbright and appetitive summer—Esther, you, and Nathaniel—came undone, seemingly as an echo of the expanding crisis, the end of prosperity, the collapse of your dreams for a *capitalism with a human face*, a new way of thinking about life and organizing time, distributing wealth, and making use of the Earth . . .

I'm leaving you

said Gatsby to the father of the bride, *I'm through with selling off the assets of this old industry, I can't see a future for myself in these dead branches of industrial French glassmaking*; and that's when the business took a turn, the company was transformed, a shift was made toward what was just starting to be called "food processing," the power grab by industry and capital to take over land, rural areas, farms, and orchards; from the future where I look back at you, says Theseus, at the start of a century when everything is in ruins, when the soils are exhausted from following the infernal cadence of the market, when pesticides have infected the rivers and aquifers, when there is an urgent need to stop producing, stop consuming, to save what can still be saved, the lakes, the oceans, the glaciers, I hear the mother who echoes back...

I'm moving out on you too, Gatsby

you who signed autographs as Dustin Hoffman

you who stood for the future and the American Dream

my thoughts are turning away

because desire is a triangle, father, don't ask how I know this, I'd have to tell you it was from the literary studies that you thought led to the idle benches of the university and subsequent unemployment; that's when the "Stendhal phase" of your story started; do you remember, the mother, this turning point in desire when your oh-so-promising husband deviated from the sensible path your father had laid out for him?

Nathaniel the resilient, Esther's father,

turned away from his son-in-law

and Esther immediately turned away from Gatsby, whom she thought she loved

all this was to be expected

if there wasn't at the heart of this story

the death of JEROME and my collapse

I assure you, dear parents,

that I'd laugh

but though desire is a triangle and the triangle collapses when the most prominent point and the one that held the whole shape together moves away, it doesn't cause a breakup; no, the parents no longer love each other, but the family endures; the mother, instead of just voicing her feelings, starts to lie; she stays on for her boys, and friends said she showed courage; to hold on though love was waning; it would be the beginning of the end of you two as a couple, the end of projections, and the slow decline, repeatedly delayed, of the promise that you held for each other; the father of the bride, Nathaniel, allowed his son-in-law to set off on a new career; but the pact of 1969 was broken, and desire then made do with what it found: for you, the mother, a banker, let's call him *Fanfan*, who reassured you because he at least knew how to protect his loved ones; and for you, the father, "fiancées," as you called them . . . parallel lives, hidden, that nurtured your wounded ego; you, the mother, had first fallen for a man on the rise, the Gatsby of summer 1969, but your father's hard gaze and the vagaries of life had sapped his image; he was much more fragile than you'd imagined; and in this lineage that so feared fragility . . .

don't we camouflage what, from era to era, trembles in us?

and those kids, my dear little parents

an image suddenly comes back to me

those children who moved in next door

in the mid-1980s when the lie was in force

those children who watched us go by on our bikes

because we'd seen Spielberg's E. T.

and wanted, the brother and I, to lift off by pedaling very fast

those children who yelled out the window

stridently, so that the sound echoed in my ears

"LOOK AT THAT, THE JEWS RIDE BIKES!"

what was I supposed to think?

men play out the scenario of success, they hide the reverberations that come from the past; they'd be too ashamed to talk about what is missing inside them or still vibrating; and the promising trio that you formed bends out of shape under the weight of your disappointed expectations; I grew up in the midst of this deception, my dear little parents, in the midst of your silences; I am the descendant of this aborted fiction of love, this attempt at camouflage, these ancient, sacred inheritances that were hushed up; and your son, Jerome, what forgotten texts should he have translated? did not his death on that day reawaken the scandal of all that fell short in the fiction of your French marriage?

I've got no balls, he told me in his final days, back in the winter of 2005; *I have all these fears and I don't know where they come from; I've got no balls, Theseus; I can't stand up to my wife, I'm afraid but I don't know what I'm afraid of; since Nathaniel's death*—the patriarch of the family had died in 2002—*I have the impression that everything is falling; he must have been the one who kept the family together, thanks to his success, his power, and now I don't understand what's happening; I want to kill myself, Theseus, the impulse is sometimes strong; I want it to stop, but my fears won't go away; and the goddamn psychiatrist the mother's sent me to just doesn't get it; all he wants to know is: are you taking your pills? but I'm not crazy; I know there's something wrong; just think, Theseus, how our mother's been living ever since we were born; always anxious, always convinced that we're going to be hit by a truck or fall off a bridge; where does it come from, Theseus, where does all this fear come from?*

so it goes with the lineage of men who die: a fiction of strength that holds fast and then lets go . . . but again, at this point I know nothing, understand nothing, I'm like the brother, Jerome, the one who picked up on the family anxiety and dread so as to try and make sense of them if possible and lift me in the process; as I look at you, dear parents, and as I uncover the ascensional life that carried you on the day of your marriage, I am just starting to grasp what comes after joy, youth, beauty, and the great promise you held for the times to come; I tell myself I probably have something to start with; the years when love was falling away, when the lie was expanding, when what gave us existence, the brother and me, the love that is part of a child's raison d'être, got lost in myths; you were no longer *together*, but if there's one thing that the upper bourgeoisie knows how to do better than any other class it's *seeming*; and Paris helped you do it, because in that city to which we moved, lying is an art; you, dear parents, were rejoicing then that Mitterrand was still in power; it was your cohorts who wanted him, elected him, and it was your friends, your *network*, as we would say today, who came in on his coattails to assume positions of power; Gatsby was at this point far from the factories that the leftists had by then abandoned, along with the rest of the country; he took a job in the movie industry; you used to say, I think, that you worked in "the audiovisual sector," so that no one would take you for a busker; but nothing happens by accident, right? there's all this *seeming*: a *seeming* love, a *seeming* couple at dinners around town, and the father goes and gets a job in *the movies*; life has its little harmonies, no? Gatsby goes to work for Gaumont Productions, and he's sent to Italy to set up a distribution network; he butts heads with the Mafia, comes back, sets out again; you, the mother, feel that he is the one abandoning you, because you're both children and talk yourself into believing that *it's the other's fault*; it would be so much simpler to recognize that the contract of the summer of 1969 had expired, that fear had taken hold of you, that both of you had gone looking for protection, and that you now felt too alone; but no, for you, the mother...

he's the one who left

you would tell me later, after the brother and I left home and the father had the courage to get his own apartment; *he left me*, you would always say, without mentioning Fanfan, your banker friend, who, as your letters report, made love to you so well; without explaining what I find in the copies of your files I have in front of me: why he crops up everywhere in the photos of my childhood and the brother's; on Sunday walks, on vacation... there's Fanfan, a *friend of yours*, who's always around, even after your death, when he asked to see me but had nothing to say, just

I loved your mother

the presence of Fanfan, the mere fact of his being in the photos, destroys the last vestige of faith I still had in what you and the father called a home; no, you never talked about it, you the mother, never came clean about your feelings, your falling out of love even in the first years of our life as a family; and yet nothing of the fiction that you both organized "in good faith," I have no doubt, no part of this movie that so frightened you, the mother, would ever be shown to us; no, you hid all that from us, and you surely thought that it was *to protect us*; but this *lie that protects*, this imperative to *protect*, where do you think it came from?

> *they lied to us, Theseus,* my brother howled on one of the last days of his life*; the mother, playing at a goddamn ideal family; and me, like an idiot, believing it; she was doing what Nathaniel had done, who also hoodwinked the people around him; Esther reproached her father for his behavior, when she was doing the same thing with her banker; and when did all this start? do you know, Theseus? what are we supposed to make of this, brother? manufacturing a tidy little story so as not to hurt the children; oh, and then the father goes off to work in the movies; that's just what they do best, all of them, peddling their stories to look like something true when in fact it doesn't hold water, Theseus! it leaks all over the place; you remember the father and the fiancées he would bring to the opera? and the mother*

with her perfectly correct lover going on vacation with us; where can you find a goddamn thing to hold to when your childhood's built on quicksand?

I'm just giving you what I got, dear little parents; the violence of Jerome's unfinished indictments before he killed himself; I look for warmth, but where? where am I to find peace, sweetness, when there's nothing, not even a mote of solid ground, on which to put my weight; when everything collapses and falls between the pictures you left; I get it, the mother, that you are convinced, that you and the father share the conviction, that children can't be allowed to hear anything painful; love stories that end, the absurdity of their birth, when they're supposed to be the fruit of a couple's desire but that desire no longer exists; yet *desire is a triangle*, did you ever realize? and there's nothing a child can't hear if you know how to talk to them; it wasn't us who couldn't hear, dear little parents; it was you, Esther and Gatsby, who were never able to bring up what really matters, desire, death, tenderness; instead you dashed around among Paris high society talking of politics, socialism, Europe, the Cold War, and America; truth is courage, and you both preferred not to bother too much with truth; so yes, I would say that Jerome was partly right; but only partly;

it was fair for him to throw all that in your face, all those accusations . . .

why give a shit about any of it?

I told him in the last days of his life

what is truth anyway?

and isn't everything fiction in the end,

an interfusion of myths?

just say fuck all that, I advised him,

it all belongs to the past,

just leave them to their arrangements

and strike forth, brother, break off

deal with your life . . .

moving on from the mother's face finding the brother again

2017–18

I understand nothing, still nothing; I live surrounded by a pile of old letters and photographs; I read Talmaï's text over two nights; and I remembered what I'd heard one evening, from my mother's lips, about his suicide; it happened on November 30, 1939, right after the aborted invasion of the Saar by General Gamelin and the counterattack by the German First Army under Erwin von Witzleben, near the start of the "Phony War"; I know how he killed himself—a bullet in his head—but the facts of his death remained a secret; my brother, Jerome, never knew anything about it; right in front of me now, I have pictures of Jerome in our country town in the early 1980s; the pictures from my parents' wedding in 1969, of a young woman and a young man launched toward the future; but I understand nothing, I don't see what connections develop between one era and another or why it acts with a delayed effect; what light, I ask myself, can illuminate this whole archive of destruction? I look inside myself for memories, and the pain won't ease up, nothing is healing, I fall and it goes on; it's grown desperate, to the point where I wish it would die; I tell myself everything would be simpler if I could leave . . .

it's another gray winter day in Germany; the brother who is left picks out a photo of his mother, puts it on the lectern he has made, and examines it like a musician; he asks himself whether he didn't leave for the East to make himself live through those nights described in the *books of the dead* of certain religions: dwelling for a time among the shades before everything turns back to day; he has just put his children to bed—they are with him this week—and he is trying despite his failing strength not to abandon them; he makes a point of preparing their *brotbox* in the morning before they go to school; over the years, it goes without saying, he has told them the whole story, not hiding anything: Jerome's hanging, the ancestor's bullet, the child, Oved, who searched for the words to the Jewish prayer; he takes the opportunity to discuss what History destroys, far beyond wars

they live in Germany, after all,

in a country where the soil is a sedimentation

of the horrors of the century,

in a city where the few high places are a pile of ruins

"Trümmer-Berg" = "Rubble Mountain"

and tonight his children finally went to sleep; for him it means he can resume the only position still available to him; he stretches out on his bed, the pictures in a jumble around him; he thinks if he has to absorb fear it's for the kids' sake, so that they won't have to cleanse time; he hopes that, by doing his work well, he can give them a brighter life, free of the shadowy spells of the past, the boxes full of old omissions; he would also like to believe that at the start of each century time can be scoured, washed clean and rid of all that's happened; spun dry so that the gray water can run out through the holes in our bodies; every family would list its secrets: *this one was Jewish; this one tried to hide her religion; this one was excluded from the clan; this one was ripped apart by a German bomb; this one was deported to the East, to Buchenwald; this one killed himself on November 30, 1939, pursued by fear; this one slipped in his shower and died in the early 1980s, this one hanged himself from a gas pipe in the early 2000s* . . . we would toss all these shadows into the water to filter them out, to let light in; and where Theseus now lives, the hubbub of the East has quieted, down in the square with its skeletal linden trees; if he rose from bed, he could look through the window and see passersby in the December mist; but he is looking inward; he examines the photograph of his mother; under a nautically themed cap, her face delicately mirrors the shape of a sail; Esther has her fingers clenched around a line—you never say the word "rope" on a boat because it brings bad luck; but no caption survives to indicate where she is; the picture was taken on vacation, that's clear; the father liked to go sailing with his family, it gave him the sense of being in charge—*the man at the helm*—whereas once back on land, in ordinary life, Esther took the reins again; and the brother who is left, Theseus, realizes that what arrested him about this image is the mother's hands and wrists . . .

> *my dead,* he thinks, *I see them gathered in a strange grouping in the gaping hole of time where they all meet; tell me,* he challenges them, *answer me if you can: when does childhood start to tremble? when do we emerge from the fairy tales we've been told? do you, the father or the mother, have any idea? and you, the brother, what do you say, what do you see? and you, the child, Oved, who loved kings and great dynasties, when does the French fiction come to an end?*

he tucks these questions away with the realization that he can't escape, whatever he might have hoped; he imagines two different teams that might in fact help him, each stitching away with an invisible thread to soothe and cure what can be cured in him; on one side the living, on the other the dead, working hand in hand; the belief helps him: there's the first level of existence with everything that is, the streets of the East, his children, the groceries in the fridge, the walks he will take tomorrow or the day after tomorrow in the Friedrichshain park, and there's the second level where the most unbearable things like a brother's suicide or the pains that keep him from living have meaning; he hangs on to this idea of *meaning*, what the body knows—*is an injury, a wound, coded information, is it the way a body and a soul connect in order to take action?*—for matter knows more than words do, more than the mind; the strata of time deposit their sediment in the body; this is what Theseus glimpses, he has an intuition of this body-memory where there is something beyond pain to be understood; he has a vision of matter's forms melding into a single continuum, the trees, the seasons, the cycles of the celestial orbs, diseases, the dead; and if he has survived—he would like to think he has, the brother who is left—it's to discover where this body-memory will lead him; to perform this ill-paid work that may be useful to those who follow: to hear the deep connection of the living with those who have passed on and the retroactive effects that strike those who survive . . .

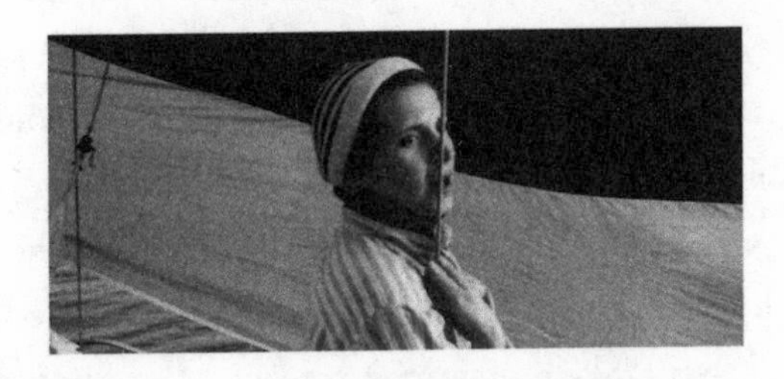

so he sticks with the images, plumbing their depths in order to force his body, oblige it to remember; and you, the mother, your hands are hanging on to a line, your face is turned to look back, full of apprehension; it helps me summon up your life, begun at the very end of World War II, April 24, 1945; you knew nothing about it, but Buchenwald, from which your uncle would return, had just been liberated; Oved and Nathaniel's brother, the third son of the ancestor who'd left without saying *farewell*; the third son would return alive, spectral in body, quiet, more mute in the art of praying even than Oved at his death; and that April 24 was also a few days after Franklin Roosevelt died, in those hours of waiting and hope when the Soviets were surrounding Berlin, while a last push brought the armies of the East and West together in the Elbe Valley for the final assault that would usher in the aftertime, reconstruction, and the Thirty Glorious Years, whose daughter you were; in this picture—there are so many I'm mainly trying to deal with the ones that strike me—your fingers on the line point me toward the brother, toward the "rope" he killed himself with; the look on your face stops me, it's a look I've often seen, anxious; in your twisting I find an incarnation of your body torn between so many loyalties; and I'll name them, Esther, so that you can see them as I do: in your youth there was a new order of women finding liberation and, soaring above, the glory of your father, Nathaniel, whose attention you sought; you wanted to be successful, make your own name famous, and yet, I watched you: all your life you waited for your father's approval; later, there was the idiotic loyalty you thought you owed your children—your two sons, Jerome and Theseus—whom you left in the care of a surrogate mother; she was the one that they imprinted on as a mother in the end, and it saddened you; because in childhood, the animal is predominant, the stomach bonds with the hand that feeds it; you worked, you came home late, you wrote your articles at night, you edited, you proofread; but what exhausted you, the mother, were the conflicts that arose from your liberation; you saw yourself as a woman advancing progress, asserting herself, but instead of finding the happy freedom of self-fulfillment you exhausted yourself trying to control everything; you wanted to protect your loved ones—your father, your children, your husband—and you were blind to what implored in you; too many men surrounded you, the mother; you fought to defend your position in journalism; and having done that you protected your sons, whom you wanted to see succeed; and there were also your brothers, who irritated you as a child, then made fun of your calling, saying *journalists are dickheads*; true, they didn't gender their criticism; when talking about women they had other words like *bitches*; do you remember, you the mother, the weight of men's looks? your brothers loved you, of course, but they didn't say so, because this family left its emotions to be expressed by the ancestor, in his Kaddish for Oved, which was never mentioned; and anyway they couldn't help it, they were boys who understood nothing about their own violence; they made comments about girls' skirts, their bathing suits, the figures of the women who walked by; they learned it in school, it wasn't that they were mean; you used the word *macho* to describe them, but it sounds so dated; in this thicket of male gazes, pre-#MeToo, you were the only girl, your father was too caught up in his work, his prosperity, his seduction, to protect you; and your mother just didn't see the importance of defending your voice; she belonged to another age, didn't feel the urgency of supporting a line of women, a power held by women, a connection between women in the world to countervail the reign and the lineage of men who die;

whereas you, on the contrary, understood it; you wanted to escape this laughter, this mockery of your brothers, these words from powerful men camouflaging fear; you wanted to fashion yourself a free life in this profession that you loved: journalism; but I saw it, Esther, you never emancipated yourself from the eyes watching you, because a reproach always bobbed back to the surface . . .

what, Esther doesn't look after her own children?

she dines out three times a week or more

never shops for groceries, takes no hand
in raising her boys

subcontracts it all to a surrogate

mother?

you're haunted by the guilt you feel for leaving your sons with a nurse, entrusting them to a substitute mom; so you phone this woman, make her your confidante; Gatsby takes no part in this, he has no idea how to boil an egg or change a diaper; the stand-in, so affectionate, so devoted, is the one your sons call *maman*, the one who's there for them, who prepares their afternoon snacks, who fetches them from school:

are they all right? you ask her two or three times a day, *are they back?* you rely on her to collect these little life moments that you miss out on by working day and night, relay them to you by telephone; and I have to tell you that this feeling, which increased in you with the years, of having walked right past the joys of daily life, when the children come home from school, when they talk about their day, and also the pleasure of watching them greedily devour whatever's put on the table in front of them, this feeling of having missed out on all these precious moments affected me so deeply that I did the opposite, my dear little *maman*

first off, don't have a career

be a household man

know how to boil an egg and change diapers

be close at hand for the little details
of life

besides, later, when everything started to darken, didn't I stay by your side? when your son died, wasn't I with you, dropping everything else I was doing? and wasn't I with the brother, too, on those days before he died? didn't I abandon my own projects when the father, at the end, needed to be bathed? in this life in the East, in this city where, unlike Paris, men and women come home from work early to take care of their kids, where you never see nannies in the park filling in for stressed-out parents, I have become a mom-guy; that's the side of the world I'm on, and I can't help looking at all the people whose jobs have them on the run, who call themselves "overburdened," as though they were possessed; I work at home, Esther; on the weeks when I have the children, I can't bring myself to turn them over to a babysitter, even for a night at the theater or to work a little longer; I am glued to the dailiness you ran away from, and it comes, I think, from my terror that my children might someday entertain a strong desire for death, for suicide, to take the place of absence

when they can no longer make out what desire or hope
gave them birth

when no one before them has done the work
of understanding the formless and violent flood of stories
that travel through us

since you left, the mother, since fate knotted the bodies of you three together, attaching them to the century we left behind, to the madness of all Europe, all the many nations, the beliefs that we stifle, the names we no longer utter, I have been watching over my children like an old wolf mother; I don't want to risk missing their fragility: the hardness of my daughter who rebelled against the cycle of bad news and knew neither her uncle nor you, her grandmother, and the fears of my sons who came after, when this whole sad inevitability was already in motion; whereas you repressed this work on the past, on private life, to devote yourself to Actuality, to High Politics; to interview the big players who think they govern and who drive our desperate growth toward more-extensive ruins . . . a sentence comes to mind when I think of all the political and business *leaders* you met in the course of your career:

"since this chaos is beyond our control, let us pretend
to be
its organizers"

that, I'm convinced, is what they do

the Great Men

whom you travel to Davos to interview, in their superprotected islands of Power

their faded Halls of State

and so I ask you, the mother, do you believe that this Actuality you served had any need of you? and the Power these men wielded, was it useful to get it on the Front Page, always the Front Page? was it necessary to waste ink and paper so we'd know a little more about what drives them, what *gives them a hard-on*, these males in search of money and recognition? don't you think History can handle our desertion? tell me, you the mother, is it worth it for an article to miss even an hour in the life of a child who is trembling? but I'm not reproaching you, I couldn't care less that you were with us so seldom; I'd even think it was a good thing if your saturated life had made you happy; if you had come to terms with being a *career girl* at least; but you had this worry, this nagging anxiety that I see in the picture, which if you'd been attentive to it would have led you to probe the shadows among which I live today; the terror that subsists at the heart of your lineage, that comes from Oved, from the ancestor and perhaps even from beyond; but instead you chased after a fault you didn't commit; and this fault, in your last months, caught up with you . . .

I haven't been a good mother

you said

I did what I could

you added, clenching your fists

if you had let go, at least, if you'd said to your sons: *you're on your own, I have my life to lead*; but you didn't want to give anything up, you wanted to be everywhere; you were scared and didn't know why, you knew nothing and wanted to know nothing of what had happened and the reason everything was falling; and even if you wanted to investigate, question the story of men's fear, you couldn't; because there's this law, the one that's governed the family since old Talmaï's suicide . . .

the windows of time are not to be reopened

so you watch over your sons' lives guided by fear; you call your confidante, your friend, the woman I should call *the mother of your children*, to know if they've been coughing; your anxiety envelops those you love; your country is a land of terror where a person might die if they were tripped, or if a branch fell on a nearly windless day; you conjure up novels in which your children fracture their skulls in tall grass, are kidnapped in a train station, get lost, or are left behind in a forest, without your ever identifying the source of your anxiety; and then there's the increasing tension between what you wanted to keep quiet and what you wanted others to believe: your perfect family, perfect children, perfect husband; you didn't realize the extent to which the hidden life you were leading, and your declining love for the father, and your unspoken love for the other one, the banker, and your fears, were pernicious

> *our mother is toxic,* said Jerome in the last days of his life, *do you realize?* and once, shouting: *for fuck's sake, Theseus, can't you see that all her anxiety over her children is destroying us? we were brought up inside her fucking fears . . .*

you would find this out in the last months of Jerome's life, when he would throw it all back in your face; it would make you collapse; but here, on the sailboat, coiled around the line—the word "rope" is never spoken on a boat—though your gaze is already tragic, you're unaware of it; you're *holding*, that's what you learned to do as a child, under the tutelage of your father, the glorious Nathaniel: you're *holding* to the point where it's harming your body; and for years medication helped you do it; there were medications to get you up in the morning, to help you interview the powerful and find an angle for upcoming articles; and there were nighttime medications to help you sleep; you were a *modern*, Esther, or so you thought at least; and the body, as far as you were concerned, was a mechanism that was meant to obey; so you pushed your body, squeezed it; and that's how you covered things for your various newspapers, right? all the divided governments, the factory shutdowns, the consequences of the fall of the Berlin Wall, the opening of Eastern Europe, the hopes for European prosperity, the unitary currency, Delors's tenure at the European Commission, the Internet, the dot-com boom; you rushed from emergency to emergency until your son hanged himself; for you, the mother, there was no sleep after that; the brother who was left, me, I remember it, I would stop by to see how you were; your face crumpled, you applied makeup to a cracked facade; it was no longer apprehension that I read there but a sense of wrong, a wrong that incised deep ravines of helplessness and shame in you; because you would have to live with the verdict

Esther, Nathaniel's daughter,

you know the one, she has the best-stocked little black book in Paris

the Journalist

who interviewed This One and That One and That Other

and profiled the minister of Finance and Economy

you see who I mean, Esther?

oh come on, you know her . . . the woman whose son hanged himself

in the weeks following that frigid day, that cursed day when my brother committed suicide, you kept saying like a possessed person, *I did what I could, I did what I could*; you gritted your teeth, *I'm going to get through this, I'm a woman who holds it together, I'm not ashamed*: that's all you learned, willpower; but now there were indictments that, as a mother, you didn't know what to do with; you went back to your newspaper, your newsroom, but the men and women there didn't know how to help you, or even talk to you; you worked hard, the mother, not to let them glimpse even the shadow of your defeat; your pride and sense of reserve bridled at sharing; after your son's death, you nourished a secret hope; you told your friend, your confidante . . .

I'd like to go to sleep and not wake up

I'd like to die

I remember our last lunch the day of your death, you tried to reassure me, *I promise you, I'm being careful*; but that was just another episode in your fiction, Esther, the nth episode of the *career girl* who dreams that everything is going to hold together, her secret lives, her career, her destiny as a mother; but I had been seeing it for months, since March 1, 2005, when Jerome, my brother, hanged himself; you couldn't think of anything but what had happened, which despite your powers as a mother, believed by you to be infinite, was irreparable; and your wish, *I'd like to go to sleep*, was granted; on January 26, when you left work at the end of the afternoon, you complained of a headache; some of your colleagues were worried as they watched you leave; you sat at the back of the No. 83 bus, and there you fell asleep; exhausted, you dropped off; I was the one the police called

is it her, they asked, *is it your mother?*

we're still waiting for the results of the autopsy
but we think it was a ruptured aneurysm

yes, a ruptured aneurysm

the day of the birth of your son, Jerome,

at the exact time that he was born thirty-three years earlier

on January 26, 1973, at the start of a crisis
that would have no end

and on some nights of the German winter, in the East, the son who is left senses that he is not going to make it; it won't be enough to listen to his wounds, to follow the ancestors' meridian, the *dai mai*, the junction line of sky and earth; *it won't work*; even if he pierces through the veil of fiction he grew up in, arrives at the other side, the second level of existence, where everything comes into focus and coheres as one story, where the fears of the ancestor interconnect with Nathaniel's, who transfers them to his daughter, Esther, who passes them on to her son Jerome by wrapping everything in silence; and though Theseus may prove the things he sees, may face the facts—*the pieces of evidence*—which are on the floor, on German soil, it won't be enough; because what's there, these spilled images, this inert mass of time that is collapsing him, is the reason why for him there's too much past and no future at all; and even though he hopes he will make it through this night, the months go by and everything is getting worse

> *these boxes of family archive,* he writes, *have weighed on my bones; I know that in other families they are kept in basements or attics; and sometimes the contents are stored on hard drives or on distant clouds, so that future people can link their names to them; we dematerialize and think to lighten; or else, in countries that put less stock in keeping the past, they destroy the archive, taking erasure for the inverted face of matter; but whatever technique is used to hold on to the past or annul it, there is this inescapable reality that makes me fall: the weight, the weight of all that now isn't . . .*

this weight, Theseus senses, is at the origin of his fall; he notices the way his body tensed as it found various expedients: flight, the multiple incarnations of forgetting; then the way he'd finally broken; he'd hoped to offer his children a new land, but he failed: the weight of memory, of what is left of his loved ones, of their absent lucidity, their unformulated fears, never leaves him anymore; discovering his family's faces, he understands that there's no other way out than to really fall, and the poor brother, this young man who has suddenly grown so old, would really like to focus on something else; his children, ongoing life, the fiery present, the future that is calling to him; he'd like to go to India or into the Mediterranean to bring first aid to this ill world; but he can no longer do anything, his body stops him, tugs on him, forces him to stay facedown...

he thinks

the body falls because trauma, the wound, is the one sense we have left

pain exists to connect us to the world

to matter

to what the body knows we don't want to see

pain is the real, the Earth,

when power has stopped

exhausting it

and now his body forces him to *reopen the windows of time*, to follow the signs that rise from his heart, lungs, spinal cord, to query the pulse that beats at his temples, solar plexus, and diaphragm, which are knotted in him to the point of suffocation; what is it that his body knows and he does not? is it this memory, this very long memory, this memory that is like the bed of a river and needs no words?

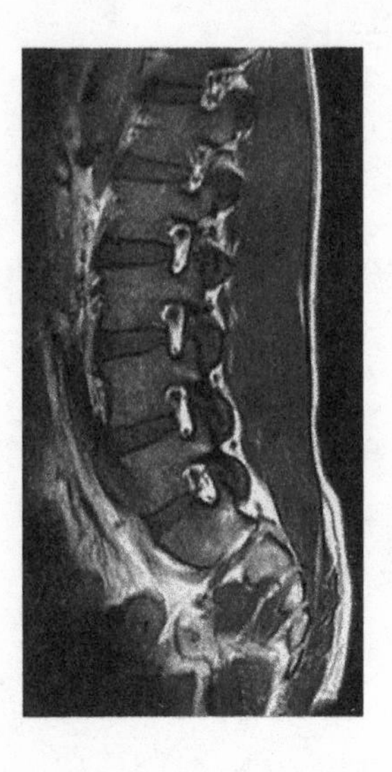

he trains himself to plumb this memory-body by listening to what is compressed inside him; to do this he learns to meditate; day by day, he becomes a disciplined soldier of attentiveness: drink lots of water, avoid all animal protein, walk even if pain keeps you from it, lie down for an hour morning, afternoon, and evening to experience the powerful art of listening; there's nothing else now: school letting out, a modest shop at the grocery store, a meal to prepare when he has the children . . . he can't carry anything now; and if you watched him walking to and from the Denn's market, you'd see him on tiptoe like an odd, ungainly bird; it hurts him to get up, hurts him to bend down; some days he has to ask for help to tie his shoes; often he slips them on without the heel; Theseus's life in the East is hard, that should be clear; an impaired dad who gets help from his children when they're in residence, who has to learn to reduce his range of movement: no looking back over his shoulder, reducing all his gestures in amplitude, hardly ever going out; he sees himself as an Oblomov of affliction; and he discovers the long voyage of those who meditate; he can no longer run or walk effectively, still less play with his children; but he consoles himself by exploring this continent he hadn't known before, which he discovers through meditation; a therapist friend is guiding him on this path; his name is Anselm, and he's managed to synthesize for his patients the disparate knowledge of integrative medicine: fasting, active listening . . . Theseus follows his guidance: he travels for hours in the position known in India as Savasana, "the corpse pose," on his back, eyes closed, arms along his body, palms up; he waits, sometimes in tears, often praying; without fully believing in it, he is counting on his body to perform the needed operations, what science calls *autopoiesis* . . .

it will take time, says Anselm; *maybe two or three years; the first thing is to free yourself of all medication; cut those out completely; and believe me, if you do this, your body will start to recruit itself; you'll see a memory-body appear*—it was he, Theseus remembers, who used this expression first—*the memory-body is what the body knows, what it gets you to discover;* he amplifies his explanation: *picture a cliff with trees growing on the top, and then imagine that your life is that overlay of trees above, while everything that's in your bones, everything that's settled over the centuries, is the rock below, the rock of the ancestors, of all the men and women before you; that's what your body wants you to discover, all that stone that's been forged around the water, the water of time flowing in you; that's why you have to follow it, watch and listen to what it knows . . .*

Anselm refuses to hear Theseus's recriminations against the father, the mother; sitting in his office, he reads him passages from Teilhard de Chardin's *Human Energy* and a later work, *The Heart of Matter*; he reads from ancient treatises on Chinese medicine; he talks to him about François Roustang, his *The End of the Complaint*; he warns him of the pleasure—the always suspect pleasure—that people sometimes take in presenting themselves as *suffering beings*; he accompanies him, imparting the technique he calls "a voyage in time"; to see Anselm navigate his initiate's knowledge so unhesitatingly, so agilely, is a new and strange experience for the brother who is left; Anselm is convinced that, using the spirit's powers, a person can reprogram his water and, in consequence, his life; for Theseus, this means exiting the labyrinth; but the pain doesn't go away, and none of what he is being taught has yet been confirmed . . .

a water molecule seen through a microscope at the moment when
a recording of the sound of the universe, Om, is being broadcast

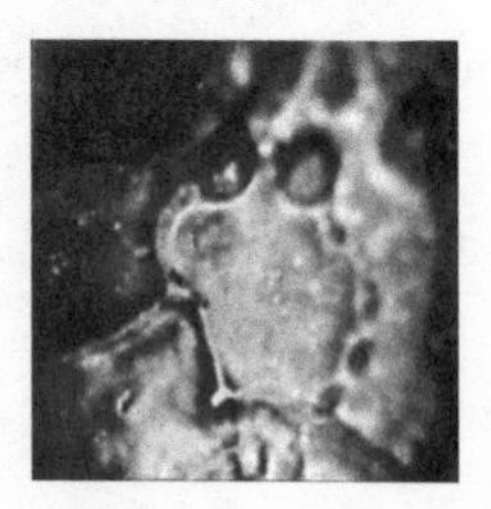

molecule of water penetrated by the howls of Metallica's lead singer

Anselm grasps intuitively the findings of Masaru Emoto, who studied the different structures of water and the variation in its crystals as a function of the information that the water is exposed to; he says that our physical matter, the physical matter of humans, *is water*, and that it's important to establish a connection with it to reshape the crystals; though Anselm doesn't express it clearly, he has absorbed this vision that life, pain, anxiety, fear, anger, hatred, and even the chemistry of what we eat—everything—informs the crystals of our water; and if we are careful to inject our water with thoughts of love and gratitude, if we nourish it with unpolluted matter, it will return to a path of greater vitality and repair the body's contaminated structures; one day, Anselm showed him a molecule of water that had been exposed to the howls of Metallica's lead singer; then another, enveloped in the prayers of Tibetan monks, water modified by "Om," the sound of the universe; and he explained that it didn't matter if he believed or not, the brother who was left, in the findings of these studies or the microscope images of water . . .

". . . our thoughts originate in the chemistry of the body

in the tensions imprinted there

we are matter that continually presents itself
in the form of language

and meditation is the art by which we leave

the bewitched enclosure of language

through meditation, we offer respite to what lives
without words,

a respite without which matter and the body cannot
find peace,

become worn, exhausted, trying to obey

words and what the mind, that evil tyrant,

dictates . . ."

Anselm adds that scientists are now studying the brains of meditators to understand how they respond to the signals they are sent; he correlates the findings of research in a number of fields, in neuroscience, oncology, cellular biology, neuronal musicology, anthropology, dietary science; he follows scientific research on the effects of fasting, the aging process, the acetone that *boosts* the fasting person's spirit; he consults articles on links between the environment, food, and the immune system; he tells the brother who is left that he will soon see the results of metamorphosis, thanks to the sustained and regular practice of meditation; he tells him that there is no other way to realize this than by doing it, day after day, week after week; so Theseus lies down and listens . . .

"water, bone water, ankle water,

water of the knees, the hips

water of the sternum, and water of the vertebrae

water of the heart . . ."

he follows friend Anselm's guidance, but still he resists; the concepts don't mesh with what he, the modern, was taught; there are always so many studies, he thinks, and the results are so often in conflict; and didn't he watch his father in the late stages of his illness put his trust in healers? yet Gatsby, his father, was not cured; the cancer took its course . . . there are many reasons for Theseus not to believe in a self-healing power, autopoiesis, nestled in the heart of living things; but he accepts it because he is not getting any better, because no doctor has managed to help him; he is ready at least to concede that he is beaten, and he is learning to relinquish his certainties; those, notably, at the basis of his faith as a modern; he reasons with himself that a living being is a vast enigma, that the links between the body and the world are infinite, that no device allows us to study them all; *he can certainly put his trust in meditation*; at the worst, it won't save him; he misses the comfort of his old confidence in science, of course, having grown up with it; that very French, very Cartesian idea that the body is a mechanism, which his mother and his father believed, living in the wake of an established dogma, care of Louis Pasteur, that pathogenic agents can be destroyed with adequate medicinal input; and when Theseus and his guide meet between meditation sessions, Anselm laughs at his resistance . . .

> *remember,* says Anselm, *that the outbreath is the most important; pause for two or three seconds; you'll find that it activates your parasympathetic system; that's the part of the nervous system that works to calm you, regulate the production of noradrenaline; if you meditate regularly, it will quiet the brain-heart links; he adds: when people are afraid, they inhale, so they are oxygenating; each time, the body gets the message to accelerate; the inbreath is the signal for*

this acceleration; it's also what we do when we drink coffee, or when we watch a crime series, getting excited in front of a television set; it draws on the sympathetic system; and often people who have a post-traumatic condition, as you do as a result of finding your brother on the floor, cut down by your father... these people don't manage to return to normal; it's like in A Clockwork Orange, *when they pry open the eyelids of that guy; you're Scotch-taped in front of a horror film and can't shut it off; it means that your nervous system can't put the brakes on; the parasympathetic side is stuck in stress mode, on constant alert; like when you tell me that every time the phone rings, you think someone is going to announce the death of a family member; you're so afraid of what you saw, you're so worried about whatever it was that took your brother, that you can't come down anymore; when I look at your EMDR results*—Eye Movement Desensitization and Reprocessing, a therapy for treating PTSD symptoms that Theseus has tried—*I see that you live on the same high level of alert as a Marine on ops...*

Ignorant, modern, beaten, Theseus has to concede that that's where he's ended up; the past is a landmine inside him that explodes, that has already taken his brother and, a little farther down the line, is waiting to take him; he's afraid for his children, though he's not sure of what; there's an alarm that never shuts off, warning of an approaching catastrophe, but a catastrophe *from the past*; from the photographs at his feet, from his brother's letters, his mother's, from what he read in the errant manuscript, which strikes him as a sorcerer's spell; so he meditates, learns to exhale; he talks to his water, while trying to silence the voices in him that object: no, he thinks, this idea of the body healing itself unaided, finding the way if given the time; I'm being had, just as my father was at the end of his life, just as my brother was; I'm reenacting the mistakes they made, thinking that they were going to get better; the father by lighting candles and learning to hold the lotus position; the brother by jumping into space . . .

the body is a machine for traveling through time, says Anselm, *listening can give you access to the information written in your deepest matter, your cells, your chromosomes; water,* he often says, *makes up seventy percent of your body weight; ninety percent of your nervous system; so what you're going to do is talk to all the water circulating inside you; and every time you lie down, train yourself to follow the water; move up from the heels, the feet, the toes, listen to the water in your femurs;*

at the same time, think of what the ancestors transmitted to you: the joys they experienced and the shocks; think of it as the hard drives of the past that are stored in you; probe these tensions at every point in your body; you've got to learn to read it like an open book . . .

this deep, other, and initiatory knowledge he is discovering strikes him as an organic poem or a prayer without dogma or ritual; he doesn't know where it's leading him, he feels motions inside him that he can't name; he realizes how completely he has lived in ignorance of this thing called "body"; he concentrates on the outbreath, as Anselm has taught him; his heart muscle hammers, his temples tambourine; when meditating, he has the impression that he is making contact with whole segments of what he has become; *a compact mass of traumatic memories and fears*; for the moment he is mostly becoming aware of what he has concealed: terrors of unknown source; while lying down, listening, he tries to slow his stream of thought; his mind is separating out, drifting away from his body; the word *fear* comes to him, and he is pulled toward memories, images; or else it's the word *anger* or *death*; in meditation he has the sense of living in limbo, a place between language and object, a point of cutoff, of disconnection; he crisscrosses the vast labyrinth within him, where the images he dreads reside; he tries to stop wanting anything, welcome absence and emptiness; he plunges into the waters of time, letting the fears of his material substance, the knots in his nerves, guide him; and there are moments when visions carry him away; for the spirit—as those who meditate know—tends to take the ascendant; and he sees the image of his brother right after his father unknotted the rope; and he realizes more and more clearly, day by day, that his nerves have re-created in him the hanged man's sensations . . .

what happens when you're there

Theseus's body asks

like the brother attached to a gas pipe?

what happens in the last moments
when the rope tightens, what muscles contract?

what do the brother's eyes see when his blood no longer irrigates them?

what do his feet feel when they hang heavy in emptiness?

do endorphins at that moment let you

disconnect from your body

as those who practice
suspension rituals claim?

do the endorphins generated release you from yourself

as Fakir Musafar reported?

do the endorphins let you see
at the distant end of the oncoming night

a flash of light?

you, my brother, did you experience the surprise
of finding the forgotten words
to the prayer?

Though Theseus tries hard to recruit his strength through this strange sleep of the body, this paradoxical sleep where the mind goes walkabout, where the nerves have time to perform their function, he is losing hope; he's afraid that his attempt to listen *from his matter* is getting him nowhere, that life is in the end just idiotic and devoid of meaning, that water doesn't follow the vibrations of his emotions, that gratitude changes nothing; neither does kindness, nor love; he's afraid he's making all these efforts in vain, and Anselm's faith in autopoiesis is a fairy tale; a beautiful fairy tale of breath and water; a myth of resurrection for the times ahead; and so he wavers between hope and defeat, between concerted effort and collapse; he'd very much like not to have to dive back into his substance but let it all ebb away and *return to life, to the present*; but he has no choice; the water, his body's water, the memory stored in his bones . . . he does everything just as Anselm taught him; then he gets up, stopping the voice of guidance, leaving Savasana, the corpse position; he raises himself cautiously to keep his back pains from flaring; and he sinks his hand again into the welter of images to see, once more engaging with his loved ones' memory, whether his pain has retreated; is he less afraid of the archive spilled out across the German floor now that he knows how to breathe?

> *I'm going to move on from your face,* says Theseus to Esther, his mother, letting the photograph fall; *I'm going to try not to think about you and your unresolved indictments; reconnect with my childhood truth; cross back through those painful years, that season of death; try not to be swept away by the emotions of the last months of your lives; by the anger you directed at the brother's wife; you blamed her for his suicide, saying that her hyperconformism, her young mother's mania for health precautions, had driven him to it; your accusations focused on their marriage, on Jerome's wife, and on the life he was running away from; but I want to move on from your indictments, Esther, your blind spots, and also from your glory years with the father, the Trente Glorieuses, when you robbed us of everything; I want to find my brother again, I want to find my childhood . . .*

Though Anselm keeps telling him to stop playing the same old record of complaint against the mother, the father, the brother—a train of analysis that tends to direct a person at and within language, focusing on the drama that surrounds every family—and though Anselm keeps teaching him that you have to deal with matter, with the body, Theseus is still dealing with family; he has to confront the images, he can feel it; there is more than water, than heart-brain connections; he has to find a home, a past, a *genealogy*, even if he has always hated the idea of it; and so he is looking for softness, sweetness, an image from the past that will give him courage; and just at this moment, a color photo surfaces among all the black-and-white ones; he picks it up, puts it on his music stand, having tossed the picture of his mother back onto the pile on the floor, and he examines it at first with a feeling of strangeness; it's his brother's face at the age of eight or nine; an age when life was still joyful . . .

> *that's what this face is,* he thinks*; a trace of indestructible childhood, before the cracks appeared that would eventually break him down; before the move to Paris that uprooted us from the forest; before we were swept up in the dark tensions of hidden arguments; before the brother started to talk like a man possessed: "I've got no balls, Theseus, I'm scared and I don't know where it comes from . . ."*

thanks to this photograph, he is able to write

I had a brother

with the sweetness you see in this photo taken by the father—almost all the photos have that sweetness, a sign that it was he who was writing the myth; a happy, adventurous myth with vacations in the sun, days on sailboats, the island-hopping exploration of an archipelago; and here, in this photograph, it's the story of father and son setting out at dawn to fish; he talked about it, Gatsby, in his farewell speech to his son in the worker-priests' chapel that the dead brother had come to love: *the chapel of the worker-priests* under the Montparnasse station, under the crowded and noisy platforms, like an unnoticed verdict on all that Jerome condemned in committing suicide: capital, power, and how a family, as a way to deal with its fear, its trembling, hid behind the protective, resilient aegis of a success story: *the chapel of the worker-priests* for Jerome, my brother, whose name, like that of my mother Esther, a woman who never acknowledged her faith, did little to indicate Jewishness, because "Jerome" refers back to the man charged with making the first translation, the abduction, of the Hebrew and Aramaic holy texts into Latin, into Christian terms . . . and so the father, on the day of the farewell Mass for Jerome, talked about his fishing trips with his son; and the brother who is left, Theseus, realizes that that's what the dead brother liked: poking around in coves with Gatsby, out of sight: the father, at other times so distant, was there beside him; fishing was a moment of serenity for Jerome, at a time when there was no serenity and no peace; because that was my brother, who was neither strong nor powerful: *he was a sweet boy*; and Theseus feels a sudden sadness when, looking at this picture, he finds that he can say

this is my brother

though he's aware that Jerome adopted many other guises, that the dead brother could be ironic, cynical, solitary, generous, or mocking, Theseus believes that these many shapes developed later; he believes that the man who in the end indicted the mother, the father, violently destroying by his death the illusion of the happy family, the man who in the end fell into his arms, sobbing, shouting: *I'm scared, I'm terrified and I don't know where it comes from, I don't know where this fucking fear comes from*, that he, too, developed later; what you see of him at the time of this fishing expedition is true; in the picture Theseus can make out the lake, the dark presence of the cliff in the background, the torn sweater; he recognizes Jerome, of course, his older sibling who was with him all the years of his childhood; but he's also aware of a distance, a strangeness; it's the veil that he's drawn between himself and his past; he can't quite connect this smile, this look of shy good nature, to an *inner memory*; it all stays sadly in the photo, outside himself; it doesn't emanate from his body because, instead of tenderness, instead of the sweet face of the boy going fishing, he sees Jerome in his final days, at home, his haunted eyes trying to focus; and in the café where he made the promise not to kill himself, where Theseus grabbed him and shook him so he would keep his word; the cold that penetrated them that day, and the loopy questions that Jerome kept asking; and then his departure, when he headed toward his empty apartment . . . and finally that afternoon when they tried to contact him, when the brother who is left jumped into a taxi and received a text saying *come, come quick* . . .

tracing back from the wound

JANUARY 2019

On winter nights, in the East, Theseus has to interrupt his investigation at times, when he feels a genealogical anger, a powerless hatred, rising in him; so he goes into the parks in his neighborhood to scream, in this city where no one knows him, where in the crush of its streets he finds alcoves of solitude, pockets of wilderness . . .

I mustn't let violence invade me

he thinks

and he walks in the German night, trying to make sense of his past, tugging on the thread of his wound; he's able to stop looking at the photographs for days, letting go the flood of fears his family left him; *to love*, he thinks, *to love my family in spite of all the weights they saddled me with*; and this hope of peace and regained love buoys him—*don't let hatred take hold, never let yourself curl up around your suffering*; but some days he doesn't have the strength to hope and tells himself that life would be simpler if he just got swept up in the family war, like the brother who is missing, Jerome, who accused the parents of every evil thing and specifically of causing his unhappiness; he could adopt this path, the defunct's, take up his accusations—*the other's fault, but what other?* he could label his father, Gatsby, old and sick, a "failure," his mother a "terminal worrier," and spatter the poison of his wound, his existential pain, in every direction; but who would he address his complaints to? who would he write now that they are gone? the soundless scream inside him—Theseus doesn't allow it to show—comes from his physical pain—why him?—and his terror; in the thirteen years since his older brother's suicide, he has felt that he's been torn from *his existence*; that same *existence* he can no longer find, now that his body gives him no peace; now that he is wrestling with his memory of Jerome, the translator, who should have sutured together all the texts of the past but who didn't keep his promise; because he gave his solemn word...

I won't kill myself, Theseus, I won't kill myself

don't worry

and above all, don't commit me involuntarily

I promise, so tell the father, tell the mother,

I'm not going to kill myself

and Jerome, committing suicide four days after swearing his oath, *I'm not going to kill myself*, had robbed Theseus of his joy, of what he had till then considered his luck; ever since, his bones have been of sand, and grief has unmade the shape he had assumed, destroying his defenses one grain at a time; he is dissolving into the night and doubts he'll one day recover the life he might have had; his older brother took away his place as the *second son*, Jerome in death being now much younger than he; and the fears of his lineage, which once weighed on his brother, have now descended on him; Theseus has the feeling he has been excised from the present by the death of his loved ones; and he holds it against them to have been so blind; to have deprived him of his best years with his children, when it should all have been vitality, and wanting, and thirst; the serial mourning has aged him, and he wonders if he is headed in the right direction looking for forgiveness; if instead he vented the accumulated violence on them, would he be able to get back on his feet? he feels that his bones are splitting, his midbody gives him sharp pains, the roots of his teeth are rotting; Theseus would need to access what his bones know, what he will later realize when he can coherently hear his memories, the movements of his blood, the energies he has held in check; but he is deaf to this thread linking him to the depths of the ages; as a child, looking at the stars or letting himself be pushed by the wind, he had the intuition of a presence; looking at the celestial bodies from his window, he conversed with immaterial spirits; he felt himself to be a tiny hyphen between the speed of expansion of the universe and his child's bed; but he spent the intervening years papering over his intuitions with a thousand modern considerations; fear, too, had buried them . . .

yet he persists

the wound must lead me somewhere

he thinks

it points out a path

and even if he were wrong

given how my body is crumbling

I have no other choice

and so, despite the vise clamping his neck—the brother's rope?—despite what's scissoring his sides and compressing his lungs—the father's unwept grief?—despite the pressure at his temples—the bullet piercing Talmaï's skull?—he forces himself to go out and walk, to aerate his mind, to expose his skin to the cold of winter in the East, to keep his legs from forgetting their learned movements: launching himself forward, reviving the hope that the earth will carry him, and pushing away the disequilibrium of living, the vertigo of existence; but Theseus is in pain, and even *walking* is beyond him; bent, broken, cracked when he leaves the house around eleven o'clock, he seems to be adding his pieced-together figure to the ghosts of the city . . .

he thinks

I've spent forty-three years

on Earth

I can no longer do anything, my whole body is crumbling

medically, Theseus has lost
eighty percent of his motor capacity

he thinks

everything is falling and life is accursed

and when he passes old men in the street, he sees them as brothers, because he now knows what it is to lose, to tremble, to limp, to see death come; like them he looks for places to support his weight, a bench, a wall to lean on; sometimes he has to carry a cane to ease the pressure crushing him; he feels the weight of several lives weighing him down, but he doesn't know how to get out from under it; he has the impression that the past is swallowing him up; during these winter months more than thirteen years after the death of his older brother, suicide beckons

suicide, he thinks, *is not an act of free will, not a social fact*

it's a solution

for freeing the dead souls that weigh down our bodies

a solution that would avoid this crossing

I must make

and he now doubts he will be able to get back on his feet

he asks himself

who teaches us to empty our bodies of ghosts,
the ghosts that stubbornly insist on living
through us?

Theseus is in the labyrinth, Theseus trembles between the laid-out bodies of the men and women who've preceded him there, Theseus hears the monster in the distance, behind a wall, waiting for him, but he keeps moving forward, not out of courage but because his body leaves him no choice; he made his brother promise, years ago, not to kill himself, to let time do its work; he wouldn't want to go against time himself now and what material existence requires; *show patience* until he experiences an inner transformation; *pass through* the fears of men; and this time, the hope he puts in matter, in *what the body imposes*, helps him endure the pain; yet there are days like this when he wants to give up; he feels the breath of surrender—*what a relief it would be not to feel*—but something in him stubbornly resists; is it his faith, in fact, that matter is God, or an intuition that what's crushing him doesn't belong to him—*old, tormented souls?*—and that he'll find a way to rid himself of them? so Theseus forces himself to go out walking, so as not to buckle; notwithstanding the pain, he walks . . . in the hope of standing upright again; leaving the house, he walks by the park where all the local children gather in the spring to laugh and play, then turns right toward Kollwitzplatz, where a sculpture awaits him; the likeness of a *mother* that this country in which he has sought refuge venerates: Käthe Kollwitz, a woman artist who lost a child in the Great War and, in a feverish Europe where young fascist extremists promised to halt decline, became a pacifist; she, Käthe Kollwitz, the very virtuous Käthe Kollwitz, who in the dark years of Germany's bankruptcy looked after orphans while so much of the country chased and desired death, looked after orphans . . .

and today, on his German walk, he hears the cries of canceled lives, which are numerous here; the voices of the disappeared mingle with the kids' voices on the *Klettergerüst*, as if his body vibrated to a frequency from the past; he walks across the gilded paving stones engraved with commemorations for the disappeared—these form the ground of the city in the East; but he still refuses to listen to the links forged in him between the ages; Theseus is a modern, he persists in being a modern, and he rejects *the invisible beings* with whom he communicated as a child; he sees only the failure of his flight, his ebbing strength, and the madness closing in on him; he walks toward the Prenzlauerallee, where the trams glide past, catching sight behind the bare trees of the Volkspark Friedrichshain, of the height he calls his *Trümmer-berg*; his *Trümmer-berg*, his Rubble Mountain . . .

so?

says the hill swollen with the past century's debris

how are your ghosts?

will you manage to walk today as far as

the summit?

. . . and before starting on the ascent, Theseus sits down to rest; in these moments, he looks for points of support, for breath; he recruits his strength by *contacting* what he has learned to identify as his "center," what's called *hara* in Japan, *svadhistana* in India, the hyphen between celestial and terrestrial energies, the meeting place of the forces of matter and spirit, below the navel, right at the place where everything in him is bending and breaking; and beyond looking for that, for his *center of being* whose great power has been described to him though he can't find it or only in weak form, he begs help from the birches, the beeches, the oaks that remind him of his childhood, of joyous times with the brother in the forest; then he asks himself what kind of prayer—a prayer to the living, to the animate and inanimate, *a material prayer*—is trying to rise in him

he becomes aware then, walking next to the fountain at the entrance to the park, that months have passed since he arrived in the East and yet he still feels just as foreign; the fountain, winterized, is known here by the name of Märchenbrunnen, with sculpted characters from the Brothers Grimm, whose tales his youngest is learning in the language of the East; he notes in passing the strangeness of this fact—or maybe it's mostly fear, a fear he cannot understand but that his body has come here to seek out, track down like the monster at the heart of the labyrinth: Germany, the German language, and these fairy tales, *Hänsel und Gretel*, *Rotkäppchen*, *Schneewittchen und die sieben Zwerge* . . .

I wanted to destroy French

he thinks

all the words I grew up in

to

hear no more talk . . . hear no more talk of them

to be reborn in another language

but what can Theseus, at this stage, attach himself to?

how can I bond with these sounds

"Trümmer-berg," "Märchenbrunnen"?

and can Theseus expect to find in this city anything other

than the trace of a vanished prayer

and Oved's memory?

in any case he starts to see that the energy of his
first months after leaving the city in the West is
gone; and his solitude here has in the end joined
his other losses; his hearth and home within
the world of sound, the names of his loved ones,
disappeared when the brother died, then the mother
and the father; to this destruction he has to add
the destruction of his language—*French*—which
was the pillar of his house; Theseus has gone so far
down the road of erasure that he no longer knows
what to connect with; he no longer has a language,
a country, a dogma, a faith; even the poor faith
of being a modern; what he finds in place of his
childhood memories—the French fiction and *success
story* of Nathaniel the glorious—is a ruined house;
and how is he to rebuild himself from these tattered
fictions, these many myths, these secrets? as the
question forms, he rises and sets forth to conquer the

Trümmer-berg, the Rubble Mountain, beseeching the trees, the snowy sky, and the frail rays of the sun...

hold on to this light, he thinks,

because it's the light of a world wanting to be born

and then

how long have I been caught in this struggle

with the past that haunts me

and also

what did I come to do here, in the city in the East, if not

to rediscover the errant Judaism of the ancestors

hauling himself painfully to the summit, he feels his heart so tight, so cold, that he can no longer manage to laugh or cry; his *dai mai*—the meridian between the top and bottom of his body—feels as crumbly as glass powder; the muscles of his legs have stopped obeying him; poor guy, he is still using the methods taught to him as a child, *Nathaniel's methods*, willpower, willpower, willpower...

stop believing in effort

he thinks

in all the dead values of my family

in the stories Power tells, hiding any fragility

stop believing in French life, in the German reconstruction

in the European melting pot and Growth

accept falling

because in French we say *tenir*, to hold, *tenir à quelqu'un*, to hold to someone, *tenir à quelque chose*, to hold to something; but what can Theseus still *hold* to, unless it's these snow-covered trees, these branches that seem to envelop him; while walking, some of the links between the body and words become apparent to him, though he can't dial back his pain; and he realizes that the language of the East has made him more fragile; using it has made him feel more and more alone, more and more off-balance and anxious; when he eventually recognizes his ties to his great-grandfather's Kaddish, the errant text in homage to Oved, he will understand just how the German language burrows down to the roots of his fear, waking deep-absorbed memories; but for right now, he can feel only his anxiety, and he looks at the naked trees to give himself courage; I see him, weaving on the path to the summit of the hill, trembling with cold, surrounded by birch trees whose counsel he would like to solicit...

why in addition to all the mourning has there had to be pain?

he asks

is there something to understand

or is it just

a memory fever carrying life away?

this morning, on the paved path that winds around his mountain, on the quilt of dead leaves, between the trees, a fine scrim of snow has settled; walking forward, he's able to imprint his footsteps on it, and he turns back after a few steps to look at his tracks

if there are footprints of mine behind me

he prays

perhaps there will also be more ahead?

the clatter of the city is smothered by the tree branches; but all this urban energy that he intuits and seeks to connect to is the energy, he thinks, of a world that exists; the proof that at the end of the longest night, everything can start beating again, living; only there's this pain in him that won't let up, and he would like for life to still be bearable; a few meters from the summit, he is struck by the tracery of a chestnut tree's dark branches against the flat of the snowy sky; the smell of the woods, the rotting leaves, the earth . . .

am I rediscovering my childhood sensations

he asks

when my brother and I would go out and play?

have I come this far to rediscover in another language

what was destroyed in mine?

you and me, Jerome,

two Jews on bikes taking themselves for the kids in E. T.

going, going

at the speed of light through the forest

right now Theseus cries at being separated from the energy of the woods; so far from his childhood with his brother, from the truth of his childhood, when the two of them would go running and playing and pedaling, while telling each other stories about the monsters that live in thickets at the end of the paths deep in the forest; this was before Gatsby and Esther tore the boys from this innocent existence, before they dragged them into their busy and omission-filled lives; and what Theseus is trying to gather, toiling over the Trümmer-berg's paving stones, is this intelligence of the body, of physical matter; the place where the wound would no longer be a misfortune but an opportunity, the thread he would pull on to finally grasp the cause of his ills and be returned to the present . . .

if I have something to learn

he thinks

if despite my many trials there's a meaning

all will not be lost

and it's because he believes in this meaning, because he clings to it, idiot that he is, clings to the crazy belief that despite all the mess, all the pain, *there must be a meaning*, that he finally reaches the top of the hill . . .

and then the brother started to speak

SPRING 2019

it's the month of May, Theseus is forty-three years old, and after long hours of train travel through forests and past lakes, he finally arrives at his brother Jerome's grave; it's a cool spring day, a few minutes by car from the Swiss border, on French soil, and he walks across the lower end of a gently sloping cemetery, a few short minutes' walk from what in his childhood was *the family house*, a paradise of lawns and rose gardens, raspberry bushes, oaks, and sharp gravel that Nathaniel created to bring his loved ones together and offer them the sweet sensation of living in a country ruled in peace and prosperity, entirely removed from the sufferings of History; and next to the town hall where his parents married in the blessed hours of the summer of 1969—one of the last summers of unending energy and French abundance—he visits the crypt where he buried them one after another, his brother first, then his mother, then as though bringing the cycle to a close his father at the end of what is discreetly called *a long illness*; on that day, too, the crests of the mountains on the far side of the lake were covered in snow; around him all is quiet; he reads, written on the stone, the brother's dates, the mother's, the father's, then draws back to sit on a ledge beside the rosebush, a spray of which arcs over the crypt; Theseus, now that he's learned to talk with the dead, closes his eyes and breathes in; he can hear what his brother has to say . . .

what meaning? *asks Jerome*

what meaning have you found this life to have?

and then

tell me, what have you learned?

I've followed you, Theseus, the dead man says; since I've been here, buried, I've seen you living by the belief that *the wound will guide us*, and I've seen you fall; I've seen you limping like an old man in the city that you chose to flee to in the East, and I've seen you cry; but what do you expect to accomplish? do you think that by giving yourself over to the wound, to collapse, you'll succeed where I failed? do you want to rediscover the prayers, brother, to become a Jewish king of Germany? do you think that language and books can make things work again? do you believe that with all that stuff, the archives, the pictures, the letters, the words that you're trying to put in place of our voices, our bodies, that you'll manage to *cleanse time*? tell me, Theseus, who gave you this absurd idea that books bring peace and forgiveness exists? do you think that Jewish life, hidden through the centuries, is what will help you heal the dead? do you really think that my name, "Jerome," inadvertently derives from our Marrano past, our fear of being unmasked? are you awaiting the Messiah, Theseus, or just an appearance from your god of the forests, lakes, rivers, oceans, and glaciers? you think that now you can talk to souls and connect with the invisible, the place where bones speak, where physical matter is one and undivided; you have this idea, I can see it, that it's your duty as a survivor . . .

put an end to what devours us and start life again

just who do you take yourself for, Theseus? do you think that my suicide and the ancestor's and the death of Oved and the fathers who tremble, the sons who die, the men who fall, that all this forms an enigma that you're here to decipher? do you think that this past, the past hidden away behind the myths of success, provides an outline for your destiny? tell me, brother, do you really think you can be nostalgic for a language you have never known? a prayer you have never learned? do you believe that the blows endured by the ancestors are imprinted into the physical matter of our bodies? are you convinced that the tissues and water of which we are made are like our Earth, which has been destroyed by the history of Power, of War, of Technology, and is heavy, full, contaminated with our wastes, but capable of interpretation by those who listen? if you've come all this way to see me, is it because you've found the answer? tell me, Theseus, has the water that you cast your mind into in meditation restored you to life? do you really think you can correct history by tapping fragility, by tapping vacillation, for the source of a second birth?

Theseus turns now toward the mountain crests, the dark blue of the lake reflecting the sky; he opens and closes his eyes and allows the trilled call of the bee-eaters to penetrate him, as though these vibrations linked to the world were an integral part of his skin; he breathes in, breathes out, and each time it's the whole world that enters him; what is the point of staying here, he asks himself, in the stony field of this cemetery? shouldn't he instead turn from the dead and plunge once more into the ebb and flow of life? opening himself to the voice of his brother from beyond the grave, he thinks of the other bodies lying under stones, of how we pay our respects to those we've loved by forgetting the vast connections that make up the whole being, turning inward to our human mourning; rather than letting our dead connect us to the Earth . . .

you've had one intuition that's been on target, brother

says Jerome

and that's the archaic belief that grips us, possesses us, although we think that in all aspects we're *modern beings*, engaged with the world; I see it now that I've died; there's this kind of continuity, you're right, and I didn't see it when I was alive; all of time is reduced and compressed in a way; the names from generation to generation interconnect, and I even have the feeling that the ancestor's skull is with us in this crypt; because the flow from age to age is beyond just us, and nothing is separate; everything intertwines; I see what you may have discovered in the "corpse position," by *meditating*; I see the dates, which are a ricochet from one life to another; the tensions that beset you in place of the old pains; and you're right, everything seems to get knotted up in a single ball; I see the generation of Talmaï, the ancestor, and the death of the child Oved, and the fear; then I see this fear taking hold of the lineage; I hear the German words, and the trembling that this language revives in you from the past; I see the Jewish name that you're not supposed to say, the memories of exile, of wandering, around the sea, and the strange desire to *become French*; I see the prayers being forgotten, modernity taking over; there are secrets in the tangled skein, and a bullet passing through a skull; and then the push after the war, after the devastation, to rise up from nothingness; I see what Nathaniel, the glorious son of the ancestor, created; his Empire, his Industry, a company to feed France; I see his strength, I see our parents, including Esther, his daughter, who embark on the future to leave the hushed obscurities behind; I see this scene of Growth, of the Thirty Glorious Years, of the European continent that hopes to be healed of its bitter identities, its mad rationality; I see the decade of the fifties, the sixties, the seventies, and the sorry mimicry of America; then the crisis hits—October 1973—and from that point on the whole glorious narrative of the social revolution, the just distribution of wealth that Nathaniel had propounded, fell to bits; and the cover-up, the widespread *deadwashing*, in the sense that we talk of *greenwashing*, disappeared; the modern veil was rent and the old wounds resurfaced in the middle of the 1980s; and shock waves from the past all suddenly fell on us, the last-born of the century; and then the vast reappearance of all that had been buried; I see it, Theseus, my brother, and all the while we, the moderns, had our eyes turned toward the future; but in their march forward, the *boomers* had forgotten the archaic: the old wounds, the fears, the forgotten prayers, and what, when we're in distress, calls to us from the pit of prayer; a connection to an integrated life, to the many pasts and futures; under the modern varnish, and you're right about this, there's a trembling life that takes hold of us, awakens us; what was the twentieth century, after all, but three generations with a strong belief in the future, until their faith hit a wall? that's the moment when we came on the scene, Theseus; we, too, wanted to invent the future, but the trembling overtook us . . .

on the way out of the cemetery after Jerome's funeral—or was it after the death of the mother, the father?—an old woman had approached Theseus to tell him that when her child died, she had entered into conversation with him; the old lady advised Theseus to do the same; she added, confidingly, that she no longer hesitated to ask her deceased son for help; *it's all right to do that*, she said, *we shouldn't be ashamed to ask the dead for help*; and Theseus had smiled, because he was still at that time a modern; but since his body laid him low and with no reasonable medical explanation available, he's had to open himself to unproven systems of knowledge; turn, in his own way, toward faith, mystery; and now, with the sun dropping behind the mountains and shadows stealing across the top of the cemetery, he starts talking to Jerome as though he were there . . .

so, *he says*, can you hear me?

I hear you, *his dead brother answers*

I'm here, *he says*, it's me, Theseus, your younger brother

I know who you are; now,
I know your name

you saw me fight like Jacob with the angel?
and the whole time I thought it was death . . .

pain, Theseus, pain is
what guides us; our pains
together form the reverse of this world
that believes in its wealth, its power

I wanted to understand why you killed yourself,
Jerome; I suppose it was an attempt
to heal; because I had to admit that without you,
without an answer to this question, I couldn't
live again . . .

and do you think that's what it is? *says
Jerome*, that the pressure in your skull
is an echo of the bullet that
burrowed into the head of Talmaï,
the ancestor? that the wound is
a sign that can be read like a
letter? what about the rope I
hanged myself with, what ill has it left
in you, Theseus?

I did what I could, *says the living brother*, my body
can no longer carry me and I have to find meaning . . .

but you could have tried something
else, *says the dead man*, something
other than prayer, or meaning,
or hope; you could have held on
to our childhood; when we were
just that, brothers; you could have
recovered the sensations of our
bike expeditions; the Jorgondases, I
remember their name, who used to
spit on us when we rode under their
windows; and the sound of *French
insults*, when we didn't even know
what being a Jew was, though we
would flip them the bird back, and
pedal like crazy to reach the forest;
you could have remembered that,
brother, our childhood energy and
how, after seeing *E. T.* we imagined
that by pedaling harder we could fly

I've erased my childhood, *says Theseus*, I've
canceled my whole left side, I sentenced it
to silence the day I saw you, my left-hander,
stretched out, stiff and cold in the apartment
with the prostrate father beside you; and
you're right, I could have held on to the joy
of our early years, but there was nothing left
of them; you took all of that away, our laughter, our
enthusiasms; every time I try to remember back,
your body after the father unknotted it turns
up from the past...

> and you think it's that? *says Jerome*,
> a meaning calling to you, the meaning
> of the forests, lakes, and rivers, the
> meaning that is in each body, each
> cell of our skin, you think pain is
> a language that we have to learn to
> read, and God is the flow of physical
> matter?

I don't know, *says Theseus*, I just think
there has to be meaning; do you know what day it is?

the dead brother at this moment seems to wander
off, allowing the full-throated roar of an outboard

motor to rise up in the air, breaking into a thousand
echoes against the walls of the mountains that ring the
pearly waters of the lake; Theseus looks up; if nothing
is sacred, he thinks, if material life is not precisely
everything that is sacred, then this world does not exist;
and Theseus gives himself to the silence of the cemetery,
turned like a theater toward the summits, the pale, icy
waters; this is *presence*, he thinks, this is the breath that
carries the world; and he finds himself hoping that it
will be even so inside him, one day . . .

the second of March, *says Theseus*, this is the
second of March; that's the date inscribed at
the end of the ancestor's manuscript; and maybe
I came here, to your grave, for that, Jerome,
to give you this text to read: "life doesn't
stop here, *wrote Oved's father, Talmaï*,
I don't plan to shut myself away in a crypt
with my son; but nor do I want to
deposit him at the roadside and
move on; come, all of you, my children,
his brothers and sisters, let us gather him in our arms,
let us carry him together through the good days
and bad on the path that still lies ahead
for us . . ."; and guess what, Jerome,
it was after writing these lines that he
dated his manuscript March 2

and what day, *Jerome asks*,
did I die?

you killed yourself on the first of March, *says Theseus*

these are just coincidences, *says Jerome*,
the first of March, the second of March

you died, *says Theseus*, just before this text
made its way to you

you're crazy, *says Jerome*

the text was written for us, the children yet to come,
but it didn't reach us; it spoke of genealogy,
of kings, of genealogical breaks, of forgotten prayers; it
spoke of mourning and hope; it bore witness to the loss
of a son; it tried to make life out of death and it was
completed on March 2, you died on March 1

more than a half century later, *said*
Jerome

we can always reject the signs we find
disturbing, *says Theseus*, can insist on being
moderns; we often do this, we disguise
our ignorance by saying: *it's a chance effect*;

we reject what's presented to us; but I
didn't have a choice; without the pain, I
would never have listened to the signs; I'd
have said like everyone else: *it's a chance effect*;
but look at all we've learned to see with microscopes,
what we've been able to hear with stethoscopes:
tools create a field of knowledge that allows us
to push ahead, to translate the mysterious; how
many things have become apparent
that we originally rejected? what I read, what I
understand from the traces you left, why shouldn't it be
just that: the signs that a yet-to-be-discovered
tool will eventually decipher?

how our bodies register gunshots
the assaults of war, fears, epidemics?

and has not bedrock registered
the folds and collapses that occurred
in distant times?

why should our human matter
made of water and of all the molecules
formed here, in this world,
be so different?

if I'd read the ancestor's text, *says Jerome*,
if I'd known more about what happened,
far off, in the other century, do you
think I would have lived?

ifs are never going to save the dead, *says Theseus*,
and there are no *ifs* for you or the father or the mother;
that's not what my investigation is for; *ifs* provide
a recourse for the living; they help us change the future,
reconfigure the past, reprogram a genealogy so that light
and a little truth can enter; see, Jerome, what shifts
for us the living when I form these sentences

if you'd known that Oved haunted our lineage

if you'd heard the story of Talmaï, our ancestor,
and the grief that overtook him

if you'd had access to all that's been repressed in our story,
our fractured story

if you could have understood our destiny as Marranos

the odyssey of secrets, of forgotten prayers

if you'd heard your loved ones' fears and could have named
the shadows

if you'd understood that Nathaniel's glory

his determination to feed the world, protect his loved ones

hid a massive fear

I searched, *says Jerome defensively*, I made
a concerted effort to discover the
origins of my fear

you searched, *says Theseus*, the way moderns do,
you stayed stuck between your accusations of the father
and the mother, behind that first veil of complaints

I remember the time I came to your
house, *says Jerome*, during the last
week before my suicide, we were
already talking about that, about
pushing our investigation further to
understand where the fear was coming
from; to understand the rot under the
varnish of our childhood

fragility, *says Theseus*; pity and a sense of love; the
Kaddish to Oved never reached its destination; and
you, you obliged me to write its story; you forced me to

pull on the thread of fragility, penetrate Nathaniel's fortress of Power; it's because you died and my body gave way that I read the ancestor's text; and from that starting point, I was able to see the fear of the sons who lost their father, the fathers who lost their sons; and beyond that to see all the things that the myth confined to silence

> do you think I died from the wars? *Jerome asks*, from History? do you think I died as a Jew? do you think I should have heard what's in my name, "Jerome," the duty to translate prayers, beliefs, and sacred texts?

looking at the dates on your grave, *says Theseus*, I realize that I am your elder now by ten years; so sit still and listen while I pass on what I've learned; I know that reprogramming a genealogy is no small thing, but admit that you asked for it; I'm now older than you, and I know the prayers . . . let me address you as if you were the second son, you who'll always be thirty-three; I've learned earthly things that no longer concern you; I learned them because all of you left me—you, the mother, the father—with the whole weight of *after*; and you know, brother, I rejected this weight, I tried to destroy it by leaving for the East; but in Germany, this country of so many ruins, where my body fell, I embarked on the quest to hear what physical matter knows and that we ignore; and I've seen, yes, Jerome, I've seen a few of the connections that we regularly overlook and that I'd like to share with you . . .

Nissim's letters

1914–18

Nissim's movements in the early part of the war are hard to follow; he was sent here and there, in the North, and in his letters he writes that the enemy was advancing; they will enter Paris, he says, it will be a long, hard haul, but he's convinced that in the end our side will win; on September 1, 1914, he writes: "Dear brother, I'm trying to get this letter to you through a friend; I hope you're well and received my postcards; physically, I'm in good shape—exhausted from the total lack of sleep but getting used to it; I can't give any details, but you'll have gathered that we are moving backward; in front of us is a cohort of the German army, and since the Belgian border we've had only Territorials to put in the field against them; still, I'm sure it will all play out to our advantage, our army needs to regroup, and I continue to be optimistic . . ."

these letters, Jerome, reached me
as Talmaï's manuscript did:

old texts to which our lives are linked
that we'd like to jettison to move forward
but that travel through the years

I'd like to have you listen to these letters
all the way to their conclusion

so you can see how the mechanism operates
in the lineage of men who die

so you'll know what kills, what drains us of our strength
and to start with, I'll introduce you to

Nissim

in 1908, Nissim had recently become French; born in Adrianople, in the Ottoman Empire, he studied at the Alliance Israélite Universelle, as did his brother, Talmaï, our great-grandfather, with whom he came to France; the two of them set off, from what I can gather, to flee an ancient tyranny, because they faced a blighted future at home, stuck in a ghetto for minorities, whereas Progress was a light that, by their reckoning, was traveling westward, a light they should follow...

do you know, Jerome, what they learned at the "Alliance,"
as people then referred to it?

they learned a language that, at the time,
claimed the right to think the Universe

and do you know, my brother,
what Talmaï and Nissim recited on their school benches
in the depths of the Ottoman Empire

in French?

"LISTEN TO THE CALL, ISRAELITES

dispersed far and wide to all points of the Earth and mixed with other nations
you remain attached by your heartstrings to the ancient religion of your fathers
however weak the link that holds you still

if you haven't forsworn your faith, if you are not hiding your religion

—think here, brother, of Oved—

if you believe your religion
should show its vitality in the rough and tumble
of the ever more fervent theories of modern society

—think here, brother, of me—

if you believe that the faith of the ancestors is for each
a sacred heritage,
that home and conscience are inviolable

if you believe that a large number of your coreligionists,
still prostrate from twenty centuries of poverty, contumely,
and repression, can recover their dignity as men,
obtain their dignity as citizens

if you believe the corrupt must be reformed and
not condemned; the blind shown the way and not
abandoned, the downtrodden raised up and not simply
lamented; that the calumniated should be defended, not
passed over in silence; that all who are persecuted should
be rescued, not simply cheered on against their
persecutors . . ."

do you see, Jerome?

Talmaï and Nissim, as children, recited the words of a call,
the call of the founders of the Alliance

who had decided to raise up men and women
from misery and ignorance

so let me name them:

Élie-Aristide Astruc, Isidore Cahen, Jules Carvallo
Narcisse Leven, Eugène Manuel, Charles Netter

idealists, cosmopolitans, without whom, brother,
I would not be writing in this language

without whom Nissim and Talmaï would never have set off

but now, after only six years of secular life in the peaceful prewar streets, studying pharmacy in Paris, the city they had dreamed of as children on the hard benches of their utopian school, a school open to the world, dedicated to the great and general cause of justice and equality, the two are separated; for the nations of Europe have decided to make war to settle which is the most powerful, most universal; which has the right, in the name of universality, to subjugate, kill, and colonize; Talmaï, our forebear, will not be drafted, and he stays behind; Nissim, though, sets off for the front to give his life; they are young Dreyfuses from the Mideast—you can think of them in those terms, brother, to draw yourself a picture; I say *Dreyfuses* because they believe in France; they are incapable of questioning it; they believe in *French modernity*, *French equality*, *French justice*, just as the founding fathers of the Alliance had taught them

". . . if you believe the principles of 1789
are an all-powerful influence

that the law deriving from them is a just law

that the example of the peoples who enjoy absolute equality
is a force

if you believe these propositions, come, listen to our call
we are founding the Alliance Israélite Universelle"

and so in that fall of 1914, a fall of vast troop movements, as the murderous war of universals geared up, and the complex, crosshatched, braided loyalties of millions of composite beings, the products of exile and colonization, commingled languages and beliefs, hopes and upheavals, were tested by nations that insisted on eroding allegiances and identities, Nissim, the *Middle Easterner*, the *Jew*, the *recent Frenchman*, the good student from Adrianople, so full of his multiple lives, aided the Territorials in the mud of the Marne; he brought recruits to the front lines as replacements for the dead; and the war was moving fast, this was a time when taxis were being requisitioned to help stop the enemy advance; Nissim writes, takes notes; we can follow him day by day, he's in Rouen, in Arras, he says that if Paris falls it won't be the end, we'll have to fight on . . .

something should already be occurring to you, Jerome,
in this revisiting of history, this long memory of bodies,
in the ancient repetition of forgotten beliefs

it's

the ancestors' powerful desire for assimilation

or should I say erasure

to

"give one's life for France"

and

forget the prayers

and do you see, brother, the shadow that issues from the deepest past
when, for survival or to integrate we renounce
the rituals that connect us to the world?

do you see the emptiness and errantry born of these deleted connections?

brother, you who are here in this cemetery
in France

do you start to understand how bodies interconnect
life after life

those two, Nissim and his younger brother, Talmaï,
our forebear,
dreamed of fighting for a nation they
had just joined

while we two,
brothers also, caught up in the flood of time
decided to run away from it

you by committing suicide, Jerome, and I
by leaving for another country

GERMANY

which, for Theseus, as I am starting to understand, is the monster at the heart of the labyrinth but Nissim is happy to fight for France, in battle he forgets that he grew up elsewhere and has ties to the "religion of his fathers"; he changes postings, worries at not receiving letters from our future ancestor, his younger sibling; he describes himself as full of energy, glad to have been reassigned from driving; he says he wants to "join the war for real" and on September 11 writes from Rouen: "I was able to take part in quite a sporting expedition, which I returned from last night; we were to blow up a railway line that the enemy relied on heavily; one hundred fifty kilometers inside enemy lines with one hundred soldiers; following country lanes, we reached our target without being spotted; it took us three hours to mine the railway, and at eight a.m. we blew it up; we were five hundred meters from an occupied village, and we learned that it was garrisoned with only fifty Germans, the rest having advanced to the front; with our commander's consent, we piled a dozen men into two cars and drove into the middle of the square; it was ten in the morning, and fifteen or so krauts were eating at tables and smoking; we opened fire at close range . . ."

do you see, Jerome, this circle that is starting to close?

why did I leave for Germany?
why did my body wait until I was settled there
to fall?

I believed, when I left, in my own freedom, in choice

thinking I was going toward the future

in a Europe emancipated
from ghosts

chance doesn't exist, brother

the body pays us no mind, steers our fate
matter is in charge, the unremembered vibrations
govern us
the buried secrets, the wounds from the past
summon us

I left for Germany to remember
the scattered, errant life

to find again the fragility
of the border-crosser

to pass through fear
and tell the ancestors: look, you who lie there
between the walls of the labyrinth

you who carry the memory of long centuries
when prayers had to be silent, when our names had to be changed
to escape being murdered

I came to end the payment of this tribute to History
our having to disappear to feed
the monster of Nations

I came, dear departed, to kill the Minotaur

and believe me, my brother

now that it's coming back, that it's reappearing, I see it:

all our beliefs as moderns will be shown false

do you see it, brother? you didn't choose to kill yourself

I didn't choose to go live in the East

we are not free, we only
believe in our freedom

look at Nissim, the Middle Eastern Dreyfus, defier of death, brother of our great-grandfather, who rejoiced in fighting for France though he knew so little about it; he took this photograph—it looks like a *fantasia*, a horseback display of the kind painted by Delacroix, *a fantasia leading the people*, captured by Nissim, amateur Middle Eastern photographer, the Orient adrift in the northern dunes; a child of the Alliance and universal Jewish education, Nissim was there with the horsemen of the Empire; he was assigned to lead a unit of North African soldiers because he knew a few words of their language; and on September 23 he writes: "In this land of mist, the spectacle of these Arab horsemen riding through the villages in battle dress is extraordinary; we arrived in Arras yesterday at midnight, and in every village we were stopped by crowds surging from the shadows to greet us; I collected a number of souvenirs, and my few words of Arabic were invaluable; after a brief vigil, we left at two o'clock in four motorcars, *gandouras* fluttering in the breeze; we managed to surprise an enemy squadron; our little expedition was therefore entirely successful; we arrived a heartbeat too late to destroy them, but we chased the unkillable Germans all morning and dispersed them in every direction; this motorcar war, I have to tell you, is great sport; we came back with lances, sabers, helmets"; Nissim continues: "not to repeat what I've already said about my health, but I am scandalously fit . . ."

do you see how our lives intercross, Jerome?

Nissim, a scion of the Ottoman Empire, fights alongside Algerian goumiers

he says little about his life before
nothing about Adrianople, nothing about the Judeo-Spanish spoken in his family

nothing about the God he is drawing away from, for he is intent on breaking off

on going forward

he believes in his future and perhaps he is already dreaming of becoming
THE FIRST JEWISH MARSHAL OF FRANCE

he says none of this, only
that he has dredged up "a few words of Arabic"
to defend France against the Germans

so, Jerome, what do you say?

who is our brother and who is our enemy?
I'm reading you these letters so that you can see who came before us

these epics of the violence of Nations
whose weight you carried

and Nissim, when the war breaks out, is twenty-eight, born four years before Talmaï in 1886; his brother, our forebear, "the one who hides," is too young and his health is frail, he will stay behind; Nissim sets off for the front enthusiastically and, in a flower-in-the-rifle-barrel vein, writes from Blangy, near Arras, on September 24: "I lead the most interesting life imaginable; the North African *goumiers* accept me, and for the past week, I have seen active duty; in Orchies, on the twenty-second, we found the Territorials wavering; we used our machine guns to push the enemy back into the woods; one kilometer to our rear was an artillery unit probing the enemy camp, and in the blink of an eye, they cleared the forest edge; I was two meters from the explosion points, and clumps of earth shot up around me to the height of a two-story house; nice work; then in the afternoon, the dance started again, but without any joy for the enemy; one of our *goumiers* covered himself in glory rounding up a handful of soldiers; he killed eleven all by himself; my mechanic, a forty-year-old Arab, killed three; I fired a number of rounds myself; but we've also lost some of ours because an enemy band, about sixty Germans, raised the white flag to sue for peace; those bastards, can you believe it, suddenly started shooting; we French responded with sustained fire, and when they came out of their holes, hands held high, we wiped them all out . . ."

Jerome, my brother

why did I ever think I could flee to Germany?

what kind of irony possesses us?

I wanted to get away from you, from the memory of your
unhanged body
behind the door, in the kitchen recess, where the father
laid you out after unhooking you from a gas pipe

"a gas pipe . . ."

is that not, there again, an umpteenth revelation
when matter, matter, matter puts in the spotlight
all that we refuse to see

my brother

I wanted to go live in the East to protect my children,
to not live in the city where all three of you died

and what about this too
why did I fall in love
with an Algerian woman

Amra, great-granddaughter of a World War I goumier

why did we, together, choose Berlin to raise
our children?

MON ORDONNANCE MESSAOUD,
SUR MON CHEVAL « KSIRI ».

it was September 25, 1914: *big news*, writes Nissim; in the mail he sends a photograph of Messaoud, his orderly, proudly mounted on his master's horse, lent for the occasion: "You can be proud of us, *he tells our forebear*, me and my brothers in the *goum*! we were sent on a mission; heading for Belgium, we left Blangy yesterday at five in the morning; I'll tell you, we advanced slowly, because there were reports that the enemy was nearby, and that march, *mein lieber Bruder*, was superb; we have three squadrons of *goumiers*; and to see the long procession of burnooses crossing the beet fields and our Arab forces penetrating the church-spired villages, you'd think it was some unlikely reverse Crusade; but the truth, brother, is that all of us here are ready to die for France, despite its unrelenting rain: Jews and Arabs, we are deliriously happy to fight for all this country offers us; and I have to say that of all the remarkable things I've seen, this moved me the most: the support given us by these horsemen from across the sea . . ."

I'm looking, brother, at the photograph of Messaoud
that Nissim took

and I'm thinking of Europe erecting barricades

I'm thinking of all the so-called souchiens,
those who see themselves as guardians of national purity

who worry about "the great replacement,"
a reverse Crusade

there are in France, in Germany, enough bones, enough blood
from every corner of the world to bring a lawsuit entitling
all the descendants of our dead to live there freely

and maybe, in the end, that's what I'm looking for
in addition to starting my life again

to plunge into the past to mobilize the dead

so they'll insist we write on their behalf
another, still unformulated history

and Nissim, after trying to measure up to the courage of the tribal *goum* soldiers—"no, they weren't there to invade France, they were there to fight beside us," *he writes*—resumes his story: "on September 25, we arrive in Orchies . . . but Orchies, you should see it! Orchies doesn't exist anymore; the bastards burned it all down, can you imagine? the church, the factories, the houses; the women and children who were unable to escape were burned alive; a woman on the curbside was crying, behind her were sections of wall belonging to her burning house; she said that her mother was underneath, that she had nothing; and the whole of the little town is like that; there are five houses with the chalked instruction *nicht verbrennen*, 'don't burn'; this was an organized, methodical burning, a pogrom against the French! do you see, Talmaï, it wasn't a Russian pogrom but a German one! this is no exaggeration, they torched everything, and it's not to be forgotten; we had to clear the road of fallen beams in order to pass, and the priest on the front steps of the church, who somehow survived, made a blessing over us; I swear to you, *he writes his younger brother*, after seeing Orchies in ashes, I made a decision; I'm not taking any more prisoners . . ."

Jerome, let me tell you where I am in my crossing,

so many tensions, so many pains have attached to me
the past pulls at my bones, weighs on my vertebrae

I feel it, from my temples to the back of my neck
the past forms a circle around my heart
the muscles of the pericardium, the lungs, even the sternum

I feel anger when I shut my eyes
and outside, in this city in the East where I live,
I hear the language of those
whom Nissim wants to destroy

"O du gräbst und ich grab, und ich grab mich dir zu"

I hear

"you dig and I dig, and I dig myself toward you"

a line of poetry by Paul Celan that just came to me

what else can I possibly do, Jerome,
to separate myself from History
to cleanse time

I abandon myself to memories

meditating

I have the idea that these war-steeped lives climb up from my lungs

climb to my throat to filter the anger

I let them do it so that it will come out, so it will let me go

so that these worn-out dead

will stop harassing me

I want you to know, Jerome,

I so hoped my children would live in a Europe free of Nations

that I've found myself praying with the words of the poem

"O du gräbst und ich grab"

and

Grab = *Tomb*

if I dig, Lord, if I dig and vanquish their fears

will it also mark the end of the old demons

the start of a new life?

that October, Nissim can't help but notice that the front is lengthening; the battle for Reims is raging, the race to the sea starts; he comes, he travels between the lines, joins observation missions, draws rifle fire but is unscathed; *with my luck*, he writes, *nothing can touch me*; he is assigned permanently to the *goumiers* and to escorting armored cars; he says: *those playthings make war fun, we cover many kilometers and from time to time have a nice Schlachtung*, he writes in German in the text, a nice massacre; now he's patrolling at Magnicourt, now sleeping in Houdain; he reassures his brother in the rear repeatedly: "I'm absolutely fine, despite the cold nights; I am remarkably dirty, having not taken my shoes off for five days; but except for the shortage of bathwater, I'm happy; I manage not to be in want of anything . . ."

then . . . "the war goes on, *he writes*, but we don't advance or retreat; there's a great deal of artillery, and it alone has any say in the matter; we're doing nothing, can you imagine? nothing but getting targeted from time to time with stupid German shells; but they won't get us, don't worry, and tonight the news is excellent; we are gaining back ground lane by lane, road by road, and we're gradually eating away at their right flank; think what it would mean, a real turning point:

it would resolve the Battle of the Aisne; but for the moment we're facing a detachment of German Guards; and we've taken some prisoners; despite the resolution I took a few days ago to massacre them, we're trying to stay human; so don't be sad, I'll come see you soon and we'll celebrate life together, brother, life! and also, please believe me when I say we are doing fine, only the horses are painful to look at . . ."

I'm telling you, Jerome

in its silences, in the folds of its memory, your body
was filled with all this past

with this unspoken task of translating between languages
between secrets

between the cursed French
and the cursed Germans

translating . . .

but how could you have known, you
in whom people only saw

the first son of a glorious lineage, the grandson of
NATHANIEL

you who, like the father and the mother, were raised in
the modern illusion

the illusion of a rupture, a break, from which
our lives launch forth

in childhood

the only models given us
were Nathaniel's strength and the Empire
he'd created

the wonderful story of the Entrepreneur who wanted to feed
France and the whole world why not

Nathaniel the resilient, son of Talmaï the fragile
the suicide

Nathaniel who, to cover his fears,
changed himself into a sugar-man, a dough-man

what do you think, brother?

the Thirty Glorious Years whose prince he was,
were they just that?
a response to the fear of being in want, the fear of dying,

the fear of war
and in the end the fear of having lost a father?

we two, Jerome,

were given only his Power, his Success, to admire
and
the French myth
that jibed with the romance of the Reconstruction

Nathaniel, the nurturing king
who took control of the fields, the grain harvests,
who offered children a transformed food
full of salt and sugar
Growth's gift, if you like, to our intoxication

and also

Jerome,

you thought, like all the men of your line,
that you had to measure up to him

Succeed, Succeed

add your name to the history of Success

you didn't understand in time that you had to throw everything over

me, right now, just one hundred years after the end of the Great War, as I reread Nissim's letters to his brother, the fragile ancestor, the concealed ancestor, I hear on the radio the speeches commemorating the war's end; one hundred years since the Minotaur ate the children in the mud of Flanders, one hundred years since Minos-like kings on all sides exacted their tributes, one hundred years during which History has repeatedly denied the war's end by exacting in the name of Nationhood, or Power, or Race or Faith, more human tributes; and on this anniversary, if you can believe it—1918–2018—a well-groomed president, a Frenchman, kissed his fellow heads of state under the Arc de Triomphe, in Paris, to the great joy of the media, who like nothing better than these consecrations because they raise viewer ratings; and the president, the well-groomed one, I hear him heroizing, glorifying, linking up in hollow words the battles of the past with the challenges of the present; I grow nauseated, brother, sick from hearing this bogus and purportedly profound lyricism; *to the dead, to the glorious fighters who gave their lives for jack-all, for the stupidity to persist, for the grand abstractions to become entrenched*... What is History, Jerome, if not the painful experience of dispossession in the name of all those idiotic and enduring fictions: "France," "Germany," "Progress," "Victory"? Theseus or I, both of us, whichever, we listen to the speech given by the young King who governs France; and we're wounded by this borrowed rhetoric on Homeland, on Memory; what does he know, this well-groomed president, about suffering? do his necropolitics serve any purpose, brother, other than to carry us further into this other, more latent war of humankind against the Earth?

we are children of Growth,
Jerome

two boys born at the end of the Thirty Glorious Years
at the start of the Endless Deplorable Years that journalists
try to soften with the term "Crisis"

as though the Crisis were a temporary thing...

we were born, brother,
after the "Meadows Report," which should have alerted us
prompted us to bring a quick end to this killing
we all refer to by the bewitching name

"Growth"

we were born, brother,
in the ruins of a world Nathaniel believed in
and contributed to building

a time of overproduction, of consumption
meant to erase the war from memory,
sink the traumas of the past
under sugar-sweet passions

a time known to all as "modernity"

but now everything is coming back

through the rope you knotted to your neck

through matter

and on October 20, in fact, Nissim writes that the glide northward is progressing; men and cars being both tired, he says: "They've sent us to Dunkirk to rest up; the town has literally been invaded by poor Belgian refugees who are a heartbreaking sight and are being evacuated; by very fortunate chance, I was able to find a bed, *writes Nissim, brother of Talmaï the fragile, our forebear*, and the layover has completely refreshed me; I am undoubtedly campaigning in privileged conditions, *mein lieber Bruder*, because our mobility with the *goumiers* allows us to go off and find comfort from time to time; so here's the news I wanted to tell you: our unit has retaken Laventie and the outskirts of Armentières; I'd been told that Lille was badly damaged; but yesterday we marched to Dixmude, and three kilometers from the village I had a chance to fire on a tethered German blimp at a good distance; I was on the road when I saw this giant bean shape looming over the trees; I quickly brought up a machine gun and fired off 400 rounds at fair range; there is a good chance that the observer was riddled, but we weren't able to stay because German shells were sweeping the road; the weather is worsening, and it's getting cold, *Nissim says to his brother*; there's a lot of rain and fog in the morning; but don't fret over it, I have what I need; I found myself an excellent burnoose in which I can sleep comfortably . . ."

you, Jerome, I saw you through your childhood
more even after
you wanted to take part in the French success cover-up
the ever-disappointed belief that Opulence, that Abundance
could return

you were chasing after Nathaniel,
after that deformed image of Glory
because no one told you what the myth was trying to hide

and we should have investigated, brother
if I'd been ready, I could have helped you

I could have told you what Power covers up
talked to you about our bodies' fragility

but these heads of state on the radio, these freaking leaders congratulating themselves by celebrating the end of World War I; these goddamned leaders, of France, Germany, the United States, taking credit for the peace, invoking men's bravery and the end of armed conflicts that their kind, yes theirs—the men and women who are drawn to power—have organized so that the Nations may triumph by swallowing up millions of young children; *children*, I think, like Nissim, who fought, drawn to the battlefield by ideals that were, unfortunately, stuffed into his head from the cradle: Progress, Liberty, Equality; look, brother, at the *goumiers*, the Jews, the Arabs, the most recent immigrants, who give themselves to a Nation that will later reject them . . .

life is topsy-turvy
and nothing can be repaired, nothing erased

we think we govern our lives with our minds,
but our languages possess us
they are woven from all the old wars

fraught with hatred and violent feelings that we learn to hide

I'm afraid of Germany, brother,
but where does that fear come from?

I listen to the heads of state congratulate each other
after saying their words

those idiots believe in their memorial ceremony

they hope
that this big edifice of words will keep the world peaceful
prevent the Nations from succumbing to madness again

but our bodies, I know something about this,
tremble at all this past history

our bodies are possessed, threatened
by dark vibrations

in Nissim's writings from the front gathered by our forebear, I find two different tones: there are the letters, where he talks about victories and shies away from making complaints; he uses copious adverbs—*superbly*, *magnificently*—which I interpret as his wanting to reassure his brother; basically, while Nissim was in the field, he was boosting morale in the rear; there is an element of bravura in it, of wanting to exhibit a kind of joy whatever the circumstances; but tucked between the letters I also find fragments of his journal; and there, it's as if you're entering the war, the "real" war: Nissim is no longer *superbly* rested; he prays for his luck to hold, he retreats from the attacker; here, for instance, on the road to Flanders, among soldiers who've been through the wringer near Dixmude, whose church is in flames; there, *he writes, all hope is gone*: "the cows are straying, the pigs squealing, the hens rustled up by the soldiers are roosting in empty houses; trees broken by the shelling obstruct the road; while I write in a ditch, explosions go off to our front; the debris falls nearby, just two meters away; I see its cloud as it falls back to Earth; toward three o'clock, there are other explosions just a few meters from my machine gun; I see a poplar on the roadside fall; luck, *he repeats*, is the main thing; twenty meters to the left or right and . . ."

Jerome, my brother,
where do the fears of the old ones settle
in what corner of our bodies?

is this what the epigeneticists are discovering and explaining,
which the psychogenealogists till now
only described?

let me, for a minute, turn away from Nissim's letters
and the mud of the north country

I'd like to show you a recent experiment
conducted by a research group

think of a worm, yes, a worm

the kind you find in caskets, in mass graves,
in the tomb—Grab—*of a brother*

this worm I want to tell you about
is one that epigeneticists call

"C. elegans"

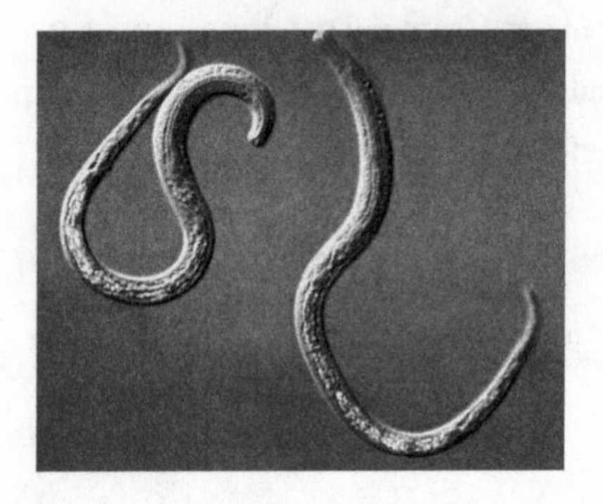

on April 21, 2017,
Klosin, A., Casas, E., Hidalgo-Carcedo, C., Vavouri, T.,
and Lehner, B. published

"Transgenerational Transmission
of Environmental Information in C. elegans"

in which it is reported that
the change in the expression of a gene caused by

A SINGLE TRAUMA

in this case, an episode of "thermal stress"

can be observed for

FOURTEEN GENERATIONS

Do you understand this, how matter encodes
the disturbances of the past, the traumas of war,
the catastrophes that Power everywhere provokes?

but Nissim, on November 6, has still said nothing about his life in the Ottoman Empire; nothing about the language he has erased, nothing about his break with the past and his departure for France; no, it is all about the Battle of Flanders, where, in these days of mud, of flooding, he has been assigned a new posting; he abandons his armored car, the regulations now requiring the engines to be armored as well, while his is not; and he joins a cavalry detachment, which occasions this beautiful passage: "I *palped* a horse," Nissim writes, "soft as barley syrup but hardy and sure-footed; he's pinched at the hindquarters, scoop-bellied, hollow-rumped, and narrow-chested; but when fully outfitted with my superb red morocco saddle with its high back and pommel, and wearing across his nose my red leather snaffle-bridle engraved with Mohammad's crescent, he almost looks dashing; he is a dark chestnut, but so sweet-tempered that we are already friends"; he has all the words at the ready, this young Middle Eastern Jew: *snaffle-bridle, pinched at the hindquarters, scoop-bellied*; the French language has taken hold in his head like a seed in new ground; a language, and a love for the Republic on the part of this Ottoman Dreyfus, now a scout in the north-country dunes; often, he says, he leaves his horse behind; he slinks between Nieuport *which is ours* and Westende *which is the Germans'*; and when you're beyond the French trenches, he writes: "You have to go by leaps, from dune to dune; otherwise you'll draw sniper fire; I have to tell you, brother, that a walk through the sands is no easy feat; everything is soaked, you see nasty things; the other day, I aimed my rifle at a bundle in the distance; with my scope, I could see two heads and prepared to fire, but nothing moved; finally I went over for a look, and it was two calcified soldiers . . ."

what do you think, Jerome?

how many generations do I have to go back
to see these TRAUMAS anchored in the physical matter
at the heart of our genes?

what kind of "worm" are we?

how many cells do we have in common
with C. elegans?

and how many shocks must I enumerate to catch
what beats, what trembles in us, what makes us die?

how many shocks from the past have imprinted in bodies,
in human matter

and should I conduct my research across

FOURTEEN GENERATIONS?

what entered into your fears, brother?

and the letter T, *through time, in the lineage of men who*
died, did it carry with it a certain drumbeat of fear?

T *for Talmaï,* T *for Theseus*

our two bodies intertangled at a distance of years

Talmaï, the ancestor, Nissim's brother, who shot himself,
and I, Theseus, whose temples are in dismal pain

could it be that the letter, the vibration of the letter
and the names, might be a sonic translation
of deeper codings?

Nissim, for his part, holds on, or I should say *he doesn't die right away*; he lives through the winter of 1914–15, describes Nieuport, which has been leveled by bombs: *you have to thank heaven when this sort of thing spares your own house*; he talks of the shadows of cooks flitting through the trenches at night, of the strange outfits of the poilus, who wear bits of finery pillaged from the Flemish hamlets; describes a dog stolen from the enemy, so riddled with shell fragments that it couldn't bark, even during bombardments; he talks of the nights when *the sublime moon* keeps him from going forward; he describes the day when, during a *djich*, a scouting sortie, after he had been crawling for an hour, he heard *Wer da?*, to which he made no answer, but it gave him the whereabouts of the enemy position; in mid-1915, he writes: *we've got the upper hand, and in the end we'll win*, and he tells how he captured a sentinel, or he describes the animals that wander onto the battlefield: *flights of pigeons, crows, and the meanderings of pathetic herds of cows*; he talks again of the dogs the soldiers send out to alert them to *djichs*; *dogs outside their lines who devour us and rip us to shreds*; he tells of the time he tried to bring back a ewe imprisoned in a hole, until his efforts came to the enemy's attention and shells started to rain down around him, pulverizing the ground; Nissim repeats himself: *the only thing around here is luck, the luck that separates the dead from the living*; and it's thanks to this luck that he gets through 1915, then 1916; mounted on horseback, he sees the long columns of stretchers; *as soon as you're away from the gunfire, war is sickening*; he pins his hopes on an expedition to Syria, on leaving the mud of Flanders to open a front in the Middle East: *just imagine*, he says to our forebear Talmaï, *the great destiny that would be: to take part in a rebellion against the Turks; to return and fight the tyrant who joined sides with the* Boches; but waiting in the *invasive mud* for this distant front to open, he laments that there is no movement: *and the waste of men's lives that the authorities are allowing, it drives me insane*; he describes the funerals of his messmates in the *goum*; also a scene in which one of the scouts, knowing he is doomed, turns toward Mecca, exposing himself to fire, to shout "Allahu Akbar": *an Arab prayer*, Nissim writes, *and a French death*; and he speaks of the discouragement in the trenches, the heroism of the Territorials: *they are really in the war, believe me . . . rotting in the wet and cold*; you get the sense that his sorties between the lines were not enough for him; he feels privileged, and though he has nearly died dozens of times, he wants to take part in *the battle, the real action . . .*

when will we have advanced far enough to go on horseback?

he writes

Nissim quickly realizes that the war will be long, too long; he cites the cold, *unendurable*, and the wind, *violent*; when the snows start to fall, *unusual seashells washed up on the beach: two Germans and two Frenchmen frozen solid*; he says again that he wants to leave the gray of the North, the mud of the polders, the sand of the dunes; the Alliance's earnest scholar who writes French with the flawless ease of a usage manual is sent on a rest break into the Flemish marshes, *which are a sea of mud*, and while there, in a long letter where we can see him trying hard not to complain, he meditates on the *horrific sacrifice* that the Nations are demanding: *what an atrocious bloodbath, my brother; the present war is claiming one hundred twenty thousand young men per month, and for what?* he talks about the propaganda, the articles in the press that brag of nonexistent lightning advances; sometimes, between the days of waiting in the rear and the nighttime outings where he manages *to kill a few* Boches, he describes a moment of grace: *you should have seen me galloping on the beach away from Dunkirk, along a delicious stretch of sea lit by the setting sun; it was one of those days, brother, when I felt sorry for the dead*; but Nissim sees the hoped-for outcome drawing farther away: the war that he'd like to wage against the Sultan: *imagine how that would be, if we could gallop with the* goum *all the way to Jerusalem*; then, coming to understand that the cavalry is no longer of any use, that *horses are useless in this battle*, and guilty at seeing the *parade of the dead* passing in front of him every day, he asks to join the infantry; unable to serve on his longed-for front, alongside a *Great Army of Arabs to establish in our native region a powerful, egalitarian nation whose minorities would have the right to live*, he climbs down into the trenches in the early months of 1917; and there, against all expectation, he continues to survive; he is more surprised than anyone: *do you realize that I am still alive? given how fast people die around here, it's an achievement*; he tells how from the moment he arrived, near Reims, his commander took a shine to him; *he's a man who has traveled, he's seen China, America, and you won't believe this but he knows the patch of ground where we grew up, Adrianople*; Nissim is spared through the unending months of 1917; he talks about Russia, whose revolution *changes the dynamics of the war, because now the Germans are going to turn their full force on us*; and then the maneuvers of 1918 start, with the Reichswehr launching an offensive to win the war outright; south of Arras in March, between Nieuport and Lille in April, north of Reims in May and June; the draft was extended, no one could really avoid it any longer; *we're holding, brother, but I'm glad to know you are in the rear; if something happens to me, you'll still be there; strangely, last night I dreamed of you with your children, those you'll have in the future; one of them was your hope and shining light; it was wonderful to see you like that, in the dream*... then, in the hours of panic when they were looking for more troops to withstand the German assault, Nissim wrote: *I see nothing but the dead, only the dead, yet no bullet has managed to hit me, brother, possibly because I'm thinking so hard about you*; finally July arrives, and from Nieuport to the very south of the front, the momentum shifts, the allied armies finally succeed in countering the enemy offensive, the front moves eastward; and right then, two days after the Bastille Day celebration, *July 14, which our teachers at the Alliance Israélite Universelle taught us to venerate*, the tide of the war turns, and Nissim is killed...

PARTIE À REMPLIR PAR LE CORPS.

Nom De TOLÉDO

Prénoms Nissim

Grade Maréchal des Logis

Corps 1e Cuirassiers

N° Matricule. 2886 au Corps. — Cl. 1914/1906
85 au Recrutement Grenoble

Mort pour la France le 16 Juillet 1918

à Montvoisin (Marne)

Genre de mort "Tué à l'ennemi"

Né le 24 Juillet 1886

à Andrinople Département Turquie.

Arrt municipal (pr Paris et Lyon). à défaut rue et N°.

you have to imagine it, Jerome,
the pain that this news caused

Nissim died at the front
in 1918

on a day when the end of hostilities was in sight

it was meant to be a last sacrifice
before peace everlasting

and Talmaï, our great-grandfather, the fragile one, survived

the two of them had left Adrianople together
to become French

but only one is left . . .

TWO BROTHERS
BUT ONLY ONE OF THEM IS LEFT

let me ask you, Jerome, in your opinion
where does his grief hide and when does it resurface?

how does Talmaï, Nissim's brother,
live through the 1920s, and then the 1930s?

with what kind of forgetting does he cover his brother's sacrifice?

and also, in this trial of mourning and separation we call

EXISTENCE

who decides where we stop and where we start

and whether we are Jewish, French, German, or Arab

who or what makes the determination?

Talmaï's suicide

NOVEMBER 30, 1939

we are lives knotted to one another, my brother; that's what happened to Talmaï, our forebear, after Nissim's death at the front in 1918; he started to condemn himself, the surviving one, the fragile one; he was ashamed to still be there when Nissim, his older brother, the courageous one, was cut down by a German shell; he was ashamed to continue as a Frenchman, when it was his brother who, since childhood, had pushed the plan of leaving for the West; he was the one, a fragile young man and short of breath, who should have died; but Talmaï survived his brother, and he had no choice but to think that he was there, on this earth, in Nissim's place; he'd followed what his elder brother had told him to the letter

find a little wife and start a family

but while his life seemed to find a meaning in the 1920s, there were questions that hollowed out deep galleries in him, forming as it were a labyrinth . . .

> *what business do I have here now that my brother is gone? what meaning does this life have if all we do is occupy the empty place left by the dead? what would I be if Nissim had not convinced me to leave Adrianople? and what about my children, must I impart to them the French myth that my brother wrote for us?*

Talmaï lived through the 1920s without answering; for a time he wanted to adhere to the myth Nissim had written, and he laid down the law that no prayers were to be said in his house; God would never be mentioned; he read his children the entire library of republican gods, Jules Michelet, Victor Hugo . . . ; he even distanced himself so effectively from his childhood recollections—erased entire areas of memory—that he wasn't worried when, after the Great Crash of 1929, anti-Jewish slogans started to reappear in the streets; he was just going about his ordinary life and congratulating himself on having *performed the mourning for his brother*; he was raising his children, having made that honorable objective his sole task; but one of them died in 1937, and that was Oved, the one who had best assimilated *the myth of France*; and from then on everything conspired to rob Talmaï of what little strength he had; he started to tremble for his loved ones and lived in a constant state of vigilance; such a mixture of terror and grief filled him that he seemed always to be *elsewhere*; after his son's death Talmaï literally didn't know what saint to turn to; in replacement for the *missing God*, he subscribed to onerous superstitions; *if I don't light this candle*, he thought, *if I put my hat on this mirror, if I keep working after the sun sets*... he obeyed Nissim, forcing himself to be a modern, but his heart was telling him different; he would have liked to believe in souls, their presence, their actions in time; then there was the day, a little shy of three years after Oved's death, when the father, Talmaï, disoriented, accompanied his elder son to the train station; it was October 1939, and *Nat*, as he was known, had been called up to the front... so there he is, the father, saying goodbye to Nathaniel on a crowded platform; Talmaï gets on the train to embrace his son, but he can't bring himself to get back off...

I'm afraid, he might say,
I'm afraid that if I let you go, the same will happen
to you as to my brother

I'm afraid of the echoes of the phrase: "letting you go"

BECAUSE EVERY SEPARATION

IS A DEATH

I'm afraid as I let you go that maybe I didn't
make the right gesture
say the right words; I'm afraid that
I didn't light the candle at the right moment
afraid that everything happening to us is
a punishment for having forgotten you

my God

but he says nothing, instead he gives the impression of being deranged; the passengers stare at him, the young men who boarded the train with his eldest almost find it funny; but no, there's no laughter; it's pathetic, and it's freezing cold; late October in France is already early winter; it snowed across the country, and the soldiers are off to another war on a frigid night; Talmaï turns toward the platform as though he might find salvation there; but salvation, alas, is not to be found on station platforms . . .

you have to get off, Papa, *the train is about to leave*
says young Nat, Oved's brother
you have to let me go . . . don't worry, everything will be fine
France can't possibly lose this war

and he adds

go, go home, they need you there
I'll be back soon, you'll see

but his father, Talmaï, doesn't get off the train; his eyes are feverish and unfocused, avoiding his son who is trying to lock eyes with him, he is *elsewhere*; now we hear the stationmaster's whistle, the shouts signaling departure; but Talmaï stays where he is, he doesn't budge, and it creates a ripple in the ranks . . .

hey, granddad, time to go!
unless you want to come with us

these are not Nat's words; no, Nat, the eldest, wouldn't talk flippantly to his father; they belong to a young blade who's having fun, who doesn't know all that can go on inside a man's skin; and at this point, every second counts in getting Talmaï off the train, but he doesn't budge; he stands there in the midst of the conscripts, who, *as always*, think that war is a party; and they see that they're going to have to help the son get his father back on the platform; that's where things stand, and you can feel the thoughts working through the soldiers' heads: Talmaï, this strange stone of a man, has to go; he needs to be pushed, they think, there isn't much time left...

the train's going to leave at any moment, Old Man!
you have to get off now...

the son tries to talk to him, begs him, *please*, so that the others feel authorized to grab hold of Talmaï and forcibly eject him; and he couldn't help himself, *he couldn't help himself*; it wasn't he who held on to a strap, at the door of the carriage, it was a *force* that was beyond him; this was on a day in October, followed by days in November when a melding occurred between eras; one Sunday, the father said *Nissim* instead of *Nathaniel* in talking about his son; and he was afraid it might be an omen; Talmaï fought against the idea, but *he couldn't help himself*; he felt that he wanted to go back to praying...

it would so simplify things to say that I need God,
that I'm not

strong enough, modern enough, to believe in the solitude and absurdity of human existence

but there's the promise between him and his brother, Nissim the courageous, which Talmaï can't break; and the memory of his son Oved, who, in his last hours, asked for the words to the prayer; and the memory of his lapse, of the vast field of the *sacred* that he was unable to supply at a crucial time when—if only for the child's sake—he should have been able to transmit a little light, the true and profound notion that there is a vast connection between one life and all others, between the dead and the women and men yet to be born, between the ancestors and the future, between pain and joy; but Talmaï remains alone, alone with the certainty that at any moment someone will bring him news of Nat's death; and alone with his fear, the terrible fear of seeing yet another connection cut, he thinks . . .

forestall grief
forestall disaster, hasten what's called a life

accelerate

finish playing the role of the father who bears up

he thinks

what freedom there would be in not holding on
in no longer being afraid, no longer pretending
no longer waiting . . .

Talmaï is alone in the living room, his children are playing outside, it's a Thursday and the weather has turned mild; on the desk, he can see several of the books that his son Oved liked to read; histories of queens, kings, emperors, and in fact France's whole glorious odyssey . . .

then suddenly there was a detonation

a single pistol shot, heard by a handful of humans

arriving out of the past, and going toward the future

thus does Talmaï die with no one around him
to understand

To Elie de Toledo,

the father who, long ago, saw his children

leave Turkey for Europe

To the men whom war, illness, and grief
carried away:

Nissim, Oved, Talmaï, and their doubles

To my brother, Jerome,

on whom so many aches, so many stories weighed

unnoticed

To the women and men whom I didn't know,

my invisible ancestors,

who, after being expelled, bore the name "de Toledo"

Spaniards, then Ottomans,

recognized as Frenchmen, denounced as Jews

carried along through the disastrous twentieth century,

whose descendants we are

Postscript

What do I know now that I didn't know before writing this story? The main thing, I'd say, is what I've come to understand about suicide, what suicide has given me as grist for thought. I'm aware that the thinking about suicide propounded in the course of the twentieth century has followed divergent paths: one line of thought portrays this act of self-destruction as a social fact; another, by contrast, sees it as a manifestation of freedom, a supreme act of self-determination. After writing this work, it seems to me that these two views—the sociological, proposed by Émile Durkheim and further developed by a large battalion of suicidologists, and the one set forth by Albert Camus and developed by Jean Améry in his valuable book *On Suicide: A Discourse on Voluntary Death*, a formulation he prefers because it emphasizes the elements of will and freedom of choice—these two approaches to suicide, whatever their merits and nuances, both entirely miss, I believe, what this book explores in the wake of transgenerational studies. These approaches also need to be reevaluated, I think, in the light of recent discoveries in epigenetics.

That said, I don't want to be misunderstood. This book does not invalidate what has been written about suicide: between *suicide as a social fact* on the one side and *suicide as a free and voluntary action* on the other, I would simply say that this story fills in our picture of the death impulse. It reveals an aspect of existence that often goes unnoticed, that of an interlaced life in which persons and their fragilities are linked across the years to one another by the shocks their bodies have absorbed. If I ask the question—Was the suicide of Talmaï the ancestor or Jerome the brother an *act of free will*?—I have to admit that I don't think so, that I consider the *act of free will* explanation to be totally inadequate. And if on the contrary I ask myself whether their suicides were *social facts*, the answer, I have to say, is also no. The traumas and trembling that attended these two suicides should point us, I believe, toward an approach that is both more historical and more material; an approach where, one day perhaps, the imprint of the trauma observed by epigeneticists in the heart of human matter will rejoin the transgenerational approaches of group and systemic-constellation psychology.

Advances in human knowledge often come about, I believe, when connections that had previously gone unnoticed are hypothesized. What can be said of the case under review? Over several generations, one's human matter is subjected to modification, buffeted by exile, exposed to deaths, births, wars, and crises. It clings to the hope of a better life and survives thanks to secrets, to erasures from memory, to camouflage. Looking at photographs of earlier times, at family albums, we encounter beings that are separated from us by decades and we ask ourselves what connection could link these lives together through so many cycles of separation. What are the ricochets, to put the question differently, of which our lives are the ripples? If we allow ourselves to enter the disquieting zone in which this book and many other elements of our collective lives have plunged me, we can ask ourselves this question, which I believe to be useful for building the new foundations that we need:

what does matter know that we as yet don't know
and that we fail to bring across the threshold of language?

What follows from this question, it strikes me, is sufficiently consequential to sweep away many superannuated certainties and frames of reference. Where, for instance, does the responsibility of a state or a business end if our bodies carry traces of inflicted violence over several generations? And if we are linked through the ages by such deep marks in our bodies, what is left of the individual, his freedom, his will? Finally, if meaning appears at the place where the wound surfaces, the pain, then what does that mean for the techniques that seek to erase them, and what are we to call what is beyond us, bigger than us, if everything is to be discovered not by lifting our eyes on high to a mystery we might call God or Meaning, but lowering them to the lowest point and accepting God or Meaning there within the sovereign and unsurpassable intelligence of matter?

That's where I am at this point. This is the question that occupies me. I haven't been able to push on much farther. I've managed to accept my brother's death, more or less. I have a better understanding of why my body started folding up, as though around a rope. I can see farther into what caused the secret and where the violence came from. And generally I remember to not be deaf to matter. My hunch is that the act of listening will provide a key: that this should push us to reattach ourselves to the world and to the lives we are connected to. And if there's a meaning to be found in our memory-bodies, in this material continuum that links our lives from age to age, I cherish the hope that, confronted with the still-to-be-collected evidence, we will consent to see ourselves, by which I mean our species, once again as humble ignoramuses before the fact of matter, which knows a great deal more than we.

that will be the start of another story

of a future that is connected

reattached